I0570906

THE GOBLIN KING

A TALE OF THE SEVEN KINGDOMS

R. MICHAEL CARD

Gryphon's Gate Publishing

The Goblin King

Copyright © 2014 R. Michael Card

All rights reserved. No part of this book may be reproduced in any form or by any means without written consent, excepting brief quotes used in reviews.

This is a work of fiction. Names, places, characters, and events are entirely the product of the author's imagination or are used fictitiously, and any resemblance to persons, living or dead, actual locals, events, or organizations is coincidental.

Gryphon's Gate Publishing

550 King St. N.

PO Box 42088 Conestoga

Waterloo, ON.

N2L 6K5

ebook ISBN978-0-9919229-5-6

Print ISBN978-0-9937651-7-9

Farion kicked his warhorse, Storm, into a full gallop and lowered his lance.

At a quick count, there were twelve goblins in the raiding party. Patchwork armor covered their gray, uneven skin. They wielded a variety of rusted weapons. He smiled under the cold metal of his helm.

This should be fun.

The creatures shrieked and ran at him. Their small, sunken black eyes gazed fury from blunt, gnarled faces.

His lance took a goblin full in the chest, but the angle was wrong, too low. With the force of his charge and the dying foe, he released the weapon as it drove into the ground.

Not a problem; he didn't need his lance to kill these abominations. Reaching over his shoulder, he drew his broadsword from his back. In one smooth motion he lopped the head from another of the creatures as he completed his first pass. The blows of the others glanced off his armor and Storm's barding.

He swung Storm around, aiming to catch the milling goblins unawares with a quick second pass. They formed up quickly though, one of them clearly giving orders in their guttural language.

Farion paused. This was new. In all his past run-ins with goblins, if there had been a leader or any sense of discipline or organization, he hadn't seen it.

He hesitated a moment longer. Something else was wrong. It came to him in a rush: armor. He'd fought a few raiding parties of goblins before and never had they worn armor. He didn't think they needed it since their skin was unnaturally tough, their bones like iron. Not that this group had particularly good armor. It looked like it was ill-fitting, scrounged or plundered from others. Only two of them had any sort of helm. The rest were uniformly bald, their ashen, lumpy scalps showing.

Armor or no, he had an obligation to take care of such invaders. He kicked Storm and swept in, sword flashing in the sun. The goblins parted, forgoing any attack. He nicked one, only from the length of his blade, but did little harm.

Storm cried out, bucking suddenly.

Farion turned in the saddle to see two goblins trying desperately to keep the hold they'd acquired on Storm's saddle and barding. Reversing his blade, he struck at each of them, wounding both enough that they let go. He rode a short distance away before turning back to the raiders.

The group was approaching slowly, warily.

The fact that they had any sort of strategy concerned

him. This was not typical goblin behavior. Perhaps the news of a new goblin king was true.

He stopped to consider his situation. They wouldn't be letting him charge through them again and again; they'd get out of the way as they had this time. He couldn't leave them be. As a knight of Lorest he had a duty to the people of the realm and there was a small village not far from here that wouldn't fare so well against even just a few of these creatures. There were two goblins down and three more wounded.

He could just wade into them and have at it...

Since no better plan came to him, he decided to do just that.

First, he made sure to lure them just a bit further away from the wounded ones, ensuring those few wouldn't be a part of the fight. Then he kicked Storm and rode right into them. They were expecting him to do another pass and separated at the command from their leader. He turned Storm to the side and reined him in as he got to the group, slashing at the same time. His blade shuddered from the force of the blow against the creature's tough bones and hide, but the creature went down, unmoving.

Only six to go.

Once he'd stopped in their midst, though, they swarmed over him. Battle-fury filled their beady eyes as they screeched in glee, their sharpened, yellowed fangs flashing.

Another blow of his broadsword felled one more, bouncing off the thing's hard skull.

So enraged were they, that some forgot their weapons

in favor of their naturally long, razor-like claws, which raked over his armor and Storm's barding. Yet others had kept their weapons. He blocked two blows from rusted swords, but felt another hack through his greave, marking his calf beneath. He cut another down before spurring Storm to get him out of there.

This time, none had managed to clamber onto the horse, and he spun around for another pass.

Time for a little trickery.

With only four left, this should work.

He charged then loosened his boots in the stirrups and, as he got to the goblins, gave a command for Storm to rear.

The well-trained warhorse stopped instantly and kicked out with his weapon-like front hooves. As Storm rose, Farion pushed himself backward out of the saddle and landed behind the horse easily.

"Attack," he said, and Storm continued to flail at the enemy as Farion came out from behind the warhorse, blade ready.

One more of the gray-skinned creatures fell before they realized Farion was on foot. They charged in, but with only three remaining the battle was soon decided. Goblins might have been tough as hardened steel but they lacked training, which Farion had an abundance. He backed off, blocking their flurry of attacks, waiting for his opening.

There it was. Stepping in with two quick strokes, only one remained.

The last, the leader—who'd been calling out the orders

until now—fled. Farion remounted Storm and ran the goblin down with ease.

He was breathing hard as he went about cleaning up this mess, ensuring each of the abominations was truly dead.

He shook his head as he looked at the scattered gray bodies marring the long green grasses of the Lorestin Plains. Goblins were trouble enough, so damned tough and furious. If they managed to get any sort of discipline, any decent training...

If the histories were to be believed, with a goblin king that's exactly what would happen. There would be a well-trained and organized force of these nasty creatures. Heaven help the Seven Kingdoms if so.

He sighed out a long breath, hoping it wouldn't come to that, and went to retrieve his lance.

The weapon had cracked from the force of that one strike and was useless.

Another sigh escaped as Farion grimaced. He hated making new lances; that was what squires were for. He mounted and continued on his way, keeping an eye out for suitable trees from which to make a new lance. He'd have lots of time to find one. He was nearing the edge of the Lorestin Plains and was still a good two days from his destination, which was well within the Everrun Forest. There'd be lots of trees to select from there.

As he rode that day, he prayed to any god that would listen that this rumor of a goblin king was only that. The foul creatures hadn't had a king in over a hundred years.

Yet with the increased raids over the last few months and how organized they were becoming, Farion was starting to have a really bad feeling about what lay ahead.

2

Farion arrived at the clearing well before noon, the sun still rising in the sky. Four others waited in the quiet glade with the distant sound of the rushing Everrun River echoing through the woods behind him. Surrounding them clustered the tall, dark trunks of maple and oak trees. The faint tweet and chirp of bird-song accompanied the rustle of wind in the branches above as Farion dismounted to greet those who had arrived before him.

Foremost among them from Farion's point of view was Legate Raithan Haldar, of the Therran Legions. Farion knew the man by reputation: a hero of the Cylean War between Therra and Lorest twenty years ago. Haldar was a legendary tactician, even if he had been on the other side. Though aged now, he was no less imposing: tall for a Therran, and stocky, with hair still mostly dark save for silver at his temples.

Raithan wore traditional Therran battle armor: light

steel breastplate over heavily padded cloth and leather tunic. The bottom of the tunic had heavy overlapping leather strips that hung to the knee, providing a good range of movement and coverage. Leather greaves and steel bracers finished the suit. The bracer on his non-sword arm had a Therran arm-shield attached to it. The shield was a hardened steel plate roughly egg-shaped and about a foot-and-a-half wide at its widest, tapering to a flared cut-out at the wrist to allow the hand maximum flexibility.

It was Raithan who had sent the summons to the other kingdoms and it was he who Farion greeted first.

Farion extended his arm for the formal Therran greeting of hand clasping. "Your reputation is well known in Lorest. I'm glad you're on our side this time."

The man's grip was like iron, the thick, corded muscles of his forearm bunching under his bracer.

Raithan's lips pressed together as he gave Farion a quick assessment. "You're Farion Quinn, yes?"

"I am."

Raithan grunted. Farion wondered what exactly that meant. It sure didn't look like the foreign general was much impressed, despite that Farion was taller by at least half a head and was in his full battle armor, freshly polished that morning.

The legate finally nodded with a curt, "Glad to have you."

Farion was sure the legendary warrior didn't think much of him, though he had no idea why. Despite Farion's height advantage, the man before him intimidated him like no other. Raithan Haldar was a name known throughout the Seven Kingdoms as one of the best generals in history. Raithan was a legend, and Farion...

He nodded and moved to the others in the clearing, making his introductions.

First was Jiska Reen, a tall Numorian woman. Next was a massive mountain of a man from Avdaland in the Far North who called himself Alred Kuronsen. Alred easily lifted Farion from the ground in an undignified bear hug by way of greeting. Last was a small woman with dark skin, which marked her as being from Mahal, the kingdom to the southwest of Lorest. She was hard in body and demeanor. Sharp eyes watched him as he approached. Most notable about her was the exposed scar on her chest where a breast used to be. The Mahali archers took their craft very seriously, getting rid of anything that got in their way including body parts. Having visited Mahal as a child, he gave her the traditional greeting. He touched his right hand to her right shoulder as she did the same.

"Hello, Lorestin Knight," she said. Her voice had a sing-song quality. "I am Krin Hana Alaui."

He knew enough of the Mahali to know that "Krin" was a rank and a high one. He nodded to her.

"Honored Krin Hana, I'm Farion Quin, Knight-Captain of Lorest," he said and stepped back, bowing low as was the customary greeting in Lorest. She nodded her head in return.

"Who else are we expecting?" Farion asked.

"As with you, I summoned one champion from each of the Seven Kingdoms," Raithan replied. The way he'd hesitated slightly before he said "champion" while eyeing Farion left a nasty bruise on Farion's ego. "Which means we're waiting on the representatives from Elrios and Tian." Raithan's tone gave the sense of speaking to a child who knew nothing about geography.

"Is there something wrong with my king's choice?" Farion bristled.

The Therran legate shrugged. "I'm sure you're the best of his knights. I just see little benefit to having a warhorse where we're going."

"Storm isn't just any warhorse. He's the best of the best and as good a fighter as you could have next to you in a tussle."

Raithan raised a single brow.

Farion realized he might have sounded a bit defensive with his last comment, but he wasn't going to retract it. "Maybe if you'd told us more about where we were going, where exactly this goblin king is, and how in all the blazes of the seven hells we're going to get there, I would have known not to bring a horse."

"All that will be disclosed shortly. It wasn't necessary in the summons."

Farion stopped himself from shouting at the general. Instead, gritting his teeth, he buried his frustration. Turning, he sought to get away from Raithan before he physically attacked the man.

Farion marched stiffly to where he'd tethered Storm. He'd been riding hard all that morning, and the stallion deserved a rubdown. Hopefully that would help Farion calm down as well.

He unsaddled the warhorse, retrieving his brush and an apple from the saddlebags. Storm chomped down the apple while Farion went to work with the brush.

Silence settled over the glade, only the birds and the distant river contributing their comments. The sun was high now, creating a pool of sunlight in the middle of the small clearing.

As Farion worked, he took a few offhand glances at his new companions, trying to size them up as best he could. Raithan was known to him, at least by reputation, and though the man had fought on the other side in the war between their two kingdoms, his reputation as a swordsman and commander earned him Farion's respect. Though as Farion actually got to know the man, the less he liked him and the more he wanted to knock that air of smug superiority off of that square jaw.

Hana remained quite still, eyes keen, body tense and ready. She carried a small recurved horn-bow: a powerful little weapon which the Mahali had spent centuries perfecting. An arrow from such a bow could puncture armor at two hundred paces. The Mahali had a single-minded dedication to whatever craft they pursued. Hana would be a deadly foe, and he was glad she was on his side.

Alred and Jiska were unknowns. Farion had never traveled to the North, and Avdaland and Numoria were mysteries to him. Just from looking at them though, he wouldn't mind having either beside him in a fight. Alred was just massive, all bulging muscle. The axe he carried looked like it would be difficult for Farion to even lift, with a blade so large it could probably fell a horse, or a tree, or a bear, or all of the above with one swing.

Jiska had an odd-looking weapon. Farion had heard rumors of a Numorian sword staff called a Kirisan. The five-foot-long haft of the weapon was topped by a two-foot blade, sharp as they come, and the base was a spiked ball of iron. Rumor had it that the weapon came apart somewhere in the middle to become two single-handed weapons.

Jiska was a statuesque woman, tall and strong. She wore chain mail over a light padding of leather. It covered her from shoulders to mid thigh, belted at the waist. Her upper arms were mostly covered by sleeves of the chainmail. Blue markings swirled over what little of her arm was exposed. She wore bracers over soft leather gloves and greaves over high boots to her knee.

Farion had to admit that even though she wasn't his type, being a touch on the tall side, she was pleasing to look at, which was more than he could say for most men-at-arms he knew. Farion let a grin slowly spread across his face as he watched her talk in hushed tones with Alred. Perhaps this trip wouldn't be so bad after all, with companions like her.

"Is that all you men think about?" a silken voice whispered next to his ear, accompanied by a warm breath on his cheek.

Farion nearly leapt out of his skin.

Within the span of his next heartbeat, even as his head turned to see who this new voice could be, two thoughts bounced around in his head. The first: even if he hadn't heard this person approaching from behind, Storm was a combat-trained horse and should have been able to see or hear anyone approaching—but the horse had not reacted at all. The second thought: how the hell did she know what he was thinking?

He turned to find a face only inches from his own.

She was exceptionally beautiful: bronze skin, thick black waves of hair cut to the shoulders, eyes the color of shelled almonds—clear and mischievous—and full lips curled into a slight smile. A straight nose and high cheeks completed the look.

"What did you do to my horse?" He hadn't meant for the harsh, accusatory tone to be quite so loud, and now everyone looked at him with curious expressions.

The woman next to him laughed, a light and airy sound. "Storm is fine. I merely calmed him so he wouldn't alert you."

How did she know Storm's name?

She turned from him, stepped around Storm into the small pool of light, and bowed to the rest of the group. Her raven hair glistened red in the radiance of the noonday sun.

"Hello to all. I'm Veyline Pristal, Mageblade of the First Order, of Elrios. I'm here in response to the summons."

Raithan nodded and strode the few steps across the glade, extending a hand. "It'll be good to have a little magic on our side. Well met."

She took his hand and they shook briefly in the Therran style.

Farion moved around his horse to be the next to introduce himself, but her next words halted him.

"Well met, Legate Haldar. Also well met, Alred Kuronsen, Jiska Reen, Krin Hana, and—" turning to him with a widening grin, "—Lord Farion Quin."

"How...?" The word escaped his lips just about the time his brain was catching up with what was going on.

He knew before she even said it. "Magic," she whispered, though the word reached all of them easily. "I don't like to enter a situation unprepared, so I took a moment to walk around the group of you and skim a little off the tops of your thoughts. Very enlightening." This last was again directed at Farion, who, for the life of him, almost blushed. No one made him blush, ever!

Gods! This morning was not going well at all.

Farion took a moment, drew in a long, deep breath, stood a little straighter, and then bowed with all his courtly training. "Well met, Mageblade Pristal."

The other three came over and offered their own greetings. Alred gave her a massive bear-hug, as he had done with Farion.

"Great to meet ya!" the big Avdalander offered.

"And you," Veyline replied.

Jiska offered a graceful bend of her knee with a slight bow of her head. Hana and Veyline touched shoulders, exchanging solemn glances.

Jiska, silent, appraised the newcomer.

Farion did the same and liked what he saw. Veyline wore no armor but was covered neck to toe in black. A light silken shirt altered between billowing with the breeze and settling on her feminine form. Veyline possessed of slightly sloped shoulders, slender arms, and small hands with fine fingers encased in tight black gloves. Soft leather pants clung to her hips and legs snugly, descending into black leather boots. He looked up and realized that Veyline was watching him appraise her.

He offered her his winningest smile.

She let her eyes wander over him for a moment. When her gaze met his again, she gave a half-smile, shrugged, and turned away.

Farion's heart fell. He didn't know why it was falling, but it was. He sighed and turned away, going to tend to Storm.

Gods! Who was this woman who could completely flummox him with just a look? His stomach churned. His face flushed. Though very upset with her at the moment, he wondered why he had such a strong urge to charge over and kiss her. Maybe that was why he was upset with her? He'd never wanted to do that with any other woman. He resisted the impulse to release his emotions in a wordless bellow. Instead, he gritted his teeth and forced his feelings down.

He heard Veyline's words to the group somewhere behind him. "Are we ready? I'm eager to be underway."

"We wait only on two more." This from Raithan.

Two? By Farion's count, only a Tianese representative should be expected. Who could be the other?

"No, we're all here."

Farion spun at the new voice behind him. That made two surprises from behind in one day.

The newcomer was small; in fact, she looked like a child. Though after a more careful examination, he had to re-assess that thought. She wore the bloom of womanhood, even if it was perhaps a recent bloom. She had hair so blond as to be almost white with a bluish sheen to it. It was cut very short to just below her ears, which was odd for most women. Her face, like the rest of her, was small with a pointed nose, high cheeks, a tiny mouth, and a sharp chin. A slender neck disappeared into a simple tunic of green and brown, which covered a slight torso and slim hips, and fell to mid-thigh. A belt around her waist showed just how tiny a waist it was. Her arms and legs were bare and pale, and she wore tight low boots of soft leather. It was her eyes and ears that gave her away. Where everything else about her was diminutive, they were on the larger side. Her eyes seemed slightly too big for the rest of her, keen and silver-blue. The ears were lobeless and protruded up from her hair a couple inches to a tapered point.

An elf?

He'd never met one and hadn't realized they were so small.

She continued speaking. "The Tianese member arrived not long ago and has been sitting in that tree observing the rest of you." She pointed upward and everyone looked.

Farion didn't see anything at first, only the faint sway of the trees in the warm breeze. Then something moved— something too big to be a bird.

A large, dark shape dropped to the ground. It landed with an easy roll and came effortlessly to its feet.

He was short, perhaps not even as tall as Krin Hana. Though slight of build, he was stocky, with many rolling muscles under his tight shirt. He had black hair, dark eyes —which took everything in at once—a slightly blunted nose, and a wide mouth, which smiled as he nodded to each of them in turn.

"Soa Li Tan, Master of Five Styles, Leader of the Armies of Liberation of Tian." It was well known throughout the Seven Kingdoms that the Tianese used their family name first, so Li Tan was his given name. The Tianese man gave a stiff bow from the waist, hands together in front of him. All in all, he didn't seem that imposing or threatening or dangerous. He was agile and well built, as witnessed by his athletic ability in leaping down from that tree—or getting up there and staying so still in the first place—but he seemed rather unassuming.

"Did you say 'Leader of the Armies of Liberation'?" Raithan asked.

"I did." His speech of the common tongue was accented heavily, but he spoke with a precision and enunciation which made his words sharp and clear.

"I've heard there's civil war in Tian, or at least, the beginnings of such. I didn't send my message to you. I sent it to the emperor and the Council of the Wise," Raithan said, a definite edge to his voice.

"You did." Li Tan was being quite close-mouthed about how he'd come to be here.

"I doubt the government would send you as their envoy if you're the leader of their internal rivals. So how did you get here?"

"If the government knew who I was, I'm sure they would have been happy to send me If only to get rid of me. When news came of your call to arms, I'm sorry to say it was met with little regard. Tian is far to the west and troubled little by happenings here in the east. They sent you a minor warrior from a noble house, seeking fame and fortune. He wouldn't have helped in your quest. I... intercepted him on the road and... convinced him to return home. I'm here now, and you're better for it."

"That's a bold statement, little man," Alred said.

No one moved, though Farion could tell each was ready for a fight if it came to that. Tension was pulled taut amongst the gathered champions.

"Though not necessarily false," Hana piped in.

"Oh?" Raithan prompted.

Hana gave a long look at Li Tan before continuing. "He said he was the master of five styles. If that's true, then I certainly would want him on this quest, and the rest of you should pay him some respect."

"Continue." Raithan seemed intrigued by this. As was Farion. Li Tan wore a slightly amused smile. Some of the tension from just a moment before had bled away.

"Well, from what I've learned of Tian, when the Council of the Wise forbade anyone who was not of the High Families, nor in the army, to carry weapons, the peasants, led by a rather unorthodox monk, began training in a style of fighting which used no weapons at all, or sometimes weapons the simple folk could get their hands on, like staves. Over time, different styles emerged in this new type of fighting—twelve in all, if I'm correct."

"You are," Li Tan said with a sharp nod.

"The styles reflected the different strengths and abilities of the people. Some were strong but not so fast, others were agile but not tough, and so on. Each style has its own offensive and defensive elements, which can take years to learn. Masters are those who know all of the forms and moves for one style. If you are a master of two styles it reflects years of training in both. It also shows a certain flexibility and it means you have few weaknesses and many strengths or you wouldn't have been able to train in both to begin with. I've heard of some of the great monks who were masters of three styles, having spent decades in training and meditation. I've never heard of a master of five styles.

"Until now." Li Tan grinned.

"Until now. And if you are what you say, you are certainly Tian's best-kept secret," Hana finished.

"Any way you can prove your ability?" Jiska asked, her tone suggesting it would be unlikely.

Li Tan cocked his head to one side. "You're the champions of your nations, are you not? If I could best one of you, maybe even two at once, perhaps that might prove my worth?"

"I'd say that would be fair." Raithan nodded.

Li Tan smiled.

"I'm in," Alred said with a grin.

"No." Raithan held up a hand to stop the big man. "We want to test him, not break him."

Alred sighed and stepped back.

"I'll do this," Raithan said, drawing his sword.

"And perhaps the tall lady?" Li Tan suggested, pointing to Jiska.

"If you wish." Raithan shrugged.

Li Tan's smile only grew.

Farion was beginning to think Li Tan's smile might just be the most intimidating part of the man.

The two approached slowly, sword steady. Jiska spun her Kirisan slowly from hand to hand—a great defensive way to get close. Raithan moved like some great hunting cat.

The two moved to either side of Li Tan, who simply stood there, watching. Though after a moment he half-closed his eyes and drew in a long breath.

Farion knew Raithan's reputation too well. This Tianese didn't stand a chance. Master of however-many styles or no. Raithan was a finely honed, extensively trained killing machine.

Raithan struck first. A calculated lunge meant to test his enemy. Farion thought the stroke would skewer Li Tan, for the man hardly seemed to move. Somehow, the strike slid harmlessly in front, only inches from Li Tan. Raithan turned his blade and sliced, but again Li Tan wasn't there. Instead, the sword slid through space just inches from Li Tan as the Tianese master had bent himself backward to nearly horizontal.

The instant Raithan's blade was past Li Tan, Farion could see the Therran swordmaster's error. Since his blade had not struck anything, he'd put too much force into the strike and over-extended his lunge. Li Tan rolled in toward Raithan, moving with such liquid speed and grace, it was nearly unbelievable. The small Tianese man caught Raithan's sword hand at the wrist and gave a quick twist, which caused the Therran general to drop his sword. Then Li Tan dropped quickly and with such momentum that he launched Raithan over his shoulder. This move was exceptionally well timed, as Jiska had been about to attack but now found Raithan in the place where Li Tan should have been. She stopped her attack in time, backing off.

Li Tan now had Raithan at his mercy. Apparently, something about the way he was holding Raithan's wrist and twisting was causing the Therran general great pain and forcing him to stay prone on the ground.

With that same grin, Li Tan lifted his free hand and motioned for Jiska to come for him.

Farion shook his head. The more he saw the more he liked and respected this mysterious little Tianese master. He grimaced as Jiska charged in, unsure how wise a move that would be.

A booted foot knocked aside her first attack. Then the same foot caught her in the shoulder, jarring her arm and knocking her off balance. Li Tan's free hand caught hold of her Kirisan and turned it around so quickly it locked up her hands. Then before she could react, he pushed her down and to the side so she was forced to one knee, her arms bent at an odd angle.

Jiska was trying desperately to free her weapon, twisting her hands, but to no avail. After a moment, she simply released her weapon and rolled away.

As she rose, Li Tan tossed the Kirisan back to her and released Raithan. "Enough?" he asked.

"Yes," Raithan said as he rose, rubbing his wrist. "I think you've proven yourself."

"That was... no one has ever taken my Kirisan from me. Ever." Jiska simply stared at the weapon in her hands. "And why couldn't I separate it when I tried?" she asked the Tianese master.

"Two reasons. First, I was holding the separation point, and second, your arms had no strength in them from the position you were in."

"That is quite the amazing trick."

"No trick. Training and knowledge of how the body works."

"Well, still amazing," Jiska said and shook her head.

Farion had to agree.

Silence fell over the clearing as they all absorbed what had just happened. Even the bird-song dissipated and the wind died. The spot of sun in the clearing had slipped off to one side, slowly consumed by shade. The day was wearing on. As if reading his thoughts, a voice penetrated the quiet.

"We're all here, should we not get on with this?" It was a high and light voice that spoke. All eyes turned to the elf.

"And who are you exactly?" Hana asked.

Surprisingly it was Raithan who spoke. "Everyone, this —" and there was a hesitation in his voice, which was surprising for such a forward, commanding man, "— is my daughter, Orinarra."

Farion knew little of elves. He'd heard of them, but that was it. He had no idea how they greeted others. The small woman used both hands to touch her forehead and then her heart and then let her arms fall to her sides, palms open and forward. She smiled with that small mouth, her large eyes shining. Again, Farion couldn't help but think how much she seemed like a child with such an open grin. If she was Raithan's daughter she couldn't be that old, perhaps twenty or thirty at most, but she looked much younger.

"Orina to my friends, which you all shall be." Her words were formal, which could have come from Therran culture, or from elfin—which Farion knew nothing about. The name certainly didn't sound Therran.

"Now." Raithan's tone was meant to draw attention back to him, with even just that one word. It succeeded. "To business."

Farion wasn't really listening. He'd known enough men who'd found themselves unwitting fathers from maids and peasant girls to recognize a certain look on Raithan's face. It was gone in an instant as the man delved into their mission. Farion smiled. He now had at least some bit of information—and possibly advantage—over the imposing Therran general. There was some long story behind the relationship between Orina and Raithan. Perhaps Farion would see if the sprite young lady would talk about it. It never hurt to know more about your enemies... or your friends.

He drew his attention back to Raithan's discourse.

"...and it was because of Orina's news of a new goblin king that I sent the call out to gather you all here."

So, the rumors were true it seemed.

Great.

"And how did the little one come by this news?" Jiska asked. There was no ill intent in her words, as Orina was quite a bit smaller than she, and the elf didn't seem to mind, but Farion saw Raithan flinch at the comment.

"She went to the Mountains of The East and saw his armies gathering."

"Did she see the king himself?" Hana asked.

"From a great distance, yes," came Orina's response. "I couldn't get closer as his armies stretch over so much land. I could hear him though, magnifying his voice through magic. He was calling his troops to war."

"How many?" Li Tan asked.

"Tens of thousands."

The clearing fell silent; even the distant river hushed, or perhaps Farion had imagined it.

"Us against tens of thousands of goblins," Veyline said slowly. "Hardly seems fair. I don't think they have much of a chance," she finished with a grin.

Alred laughed.

"Have you fought goblins before, Mageblade?" Raithan's tone showed he hadn't much appreciated the jest.

"No, but they can't be that bad."

"They're not," Farion found himself saying. He didn't know why he'd chosen that time to speak, but for whatever reason he kept going. "They're tough as steel and fanatical fighters but ill-trained. I fought a band of twelve on my way here and came away unscathed." Mostly. His calf was still healing from the light cut that had penetrated through his greave.

"Twelve to one, and you on a warhorse. We're talking ten thousand to one. I doubt your fancy horse can charge through that many."

The man just insulted Storm.

Farion opened his mouth to rebut but was cut off by Veyline. "Point taken."

Had the mageblade just winked at him?

Farion sighed, fumed, and said nothing. For whatever reason he couldn't stand to look like a fool in front of her but always seemed to end up doing just that.

"So what's our strategy?" Krin Hana spoke up.

"The reason for such a small force is not to take on the entire goblin army. Instead we'll sneak past them to get to the goblin king's lair and kill him. Without a king to unify them the armies will disband on their own and we'll be back to facing war-bands of fifty or less."

"How can we sneak past so many?" Jiska asked, obviously a little nervous about this adventure.

"That I don't yet know. I'm hoping that with our combined skills we can find a way."

And that seemed to be the end of the questions. They all stood there for a moment soaking in their mission.

"We leave immediately," Raithan said, breaking the silence. "Gather up your things and get ready for a long march through hostile territory. If we travel light and move fast, we should get to the Eastern Mountains in about a month, hopefully less. I hope your kingdoms chose wisely. This will be no easy task. We may not all make it back from the East, but we must succeed at any cost."

For a moment, no one spoke.

The birds above were chatty once again, and a new gust of wind ruffled the leaves in myriad whispers.

Farion looked around at the others and was surprised to see expressions of what he himself felt: determination mixed with fear and excitement. These were the best of the best of the Seven Kingdoms; they would do what needed to be done and would put up one hell of a fight if it came to that, but really they all knew the odds were against them.

Finally, Alred grinned and spoke. "All right then, what are we waiting for?"

3

Two weeks later the mood of the party had gone from its somber beginning to a rather cheerful high. They were making good time, had encountered several small parties of goblins and defeated them easily, and were moving through a particularly beautiful section of the Everrun Forest. The days were fairly similar: break camp, move as quickly as they could—including a small lunch eaten while walking or during a short stop—make camp late in the day, and get what sleep they could. The watch on the camp varied from night to night with one person taking the early watch and another taking the late watch. This meant that two people were usually tired the next day, but they had three more nights of solid sleep before it happened again.

They had developed a solid formation to their march as well. Alred, with his long, sturdy, untiring legs took the lead and set a breakneck pace, for walking anyway. No one complained. The rest of the party followed along in a rough line behind him, though ranging out to the sides and staggering themselves somewhat.

Farion had found it odd that he was the only one who rode, but on asking his comrades, he discovered that none of them were experienced riders. It made sense once he thought about it. Only Lorest trained extensively in cavalry, most of the other kingdoms focused on differing variations of infantry so they would be more used to walking.

Following Alred was Krin Hana, behind and often to the side, her bow at the ready and her eyes keen. Hana's legs had to take two strides for each of Alred's, but she seemed more at home in the woods and moved easily. Much of Mahal was treacherous jungle, so this sparse forest must have seemed quite pleasant to her. Hana wore hard, bare sandals, which didn't look comfortable in the least but complemented the rest of her tough exterior. The woman's dark skin was covered in lines upon lines of ritual scars, for heaven's sake; chances were good she wasn't going to complain about sore feet.

Next came Raithan, marching quickly, eyes always ahead, seemingly on their destination. Farion and the general had not spoken much in the travels so far, and Farion was perfectly fine with that. The legate seemed a quiet, introspective man for the most part and Farion wasn't about to try to break that shell. After all he was still waiting for an apology for what Raithan had said about Storm.

After the legate came Veyline, now universally referred to as Vey. She used her magic to sense impending attacks and pockets of the enemy in their path. Farion was sure she must be using magic to keep pace as well. Every time he looked at her, which he found himself doing a lot, she seemed to be moving at a relaxed pace as if on a leisurely walk. His stomach knotted whenever she met his eyes and smiled that wicked, mischievous grin. Never in his life had he found himself off-kilter when it came to women... until now. There was something about her that drilled into him, sang to him, caused his blood to run hot. He was beginning to think maybe she was using magic on him.

Behind Vey came Li Tan, though to say that he walked wouldn't have been entirely accurate. Half the time he moved like a monkey through the trees, swinging and running along branches that shouldn't have held his weight. He called it "monkey style." Farion called it "amazing to watch." The small man always had an easy grin and a ready laugh. Farion had spoken to him a few times during their nightly camps and was starting to learn a lot about the intricacies of Tianese politics and culture. If he had thought the infighting between Lorestin nobility was bad, he was learning it was nothing compared to the mire that was the Tianese government.

Last in line was Jiska, her long legs keeping up easily with the rest. She kept an eye in all directions, making an excellent rear guard. She was a woman he could speak to easily. As a warrior first she had many a good tale to tell of battle or her dalliances with Numorian noblemen. She boasted and joked and laughed like a man, and Farion was beginning to look at her in a different light. Though now and then he couldn't help but notice the flash of her bright green eyes, or her long hair, the color of embers, a warm dark red, which bounced around her head and shoulders in waves and curls. Yet the rest of her was all warrior, square shoulders, arms firm with muscle, hands covered in hard calluses.

Farion on Storm ranged around the party and scouted ahead and to the sides.

Orina did the same on foot and seemed to see more than he did. Farion had no idea how she moved around so fast—it must have been an elfin skill—nor did he have any idea where she was at any given time. She would disappear into the forest and be gone for hours at a time, only to reappear just in front of him or Alred or others in the party to relay information. She was a rather amazing little woman. He had a nearly tireless warhorse, which wasn't being taxed much at all, to get around on and still she seemed to be everywhere and know more about their surroundings than he did.

At first he'd found Orina's mysterious comings and goings mildly infuriating. Now he was used to it and simply marveled. Yet even Veyline—the mistress of mystery herself—had worn a rather dumbfounded expression the first few nights when Orina had walked out of the forest next to them as they made camp. Farion had watched Vey night after night, not that she was hard on the eyes, to see her expression when Orina arrived. It had gone from curious to amazed and slowly grown almost to anticipation. Farion was guessing Vey was using her magic to try to track Orina and had had little luck at first. Now though, she seemed to have found something that worked and didn't seem as surprised when Orina arrived, unlike the rest of them.

Every time Farion thought he'd gotten used to Orina's arrivals, she would appear just behind him with no sound, or drop from a tree above him, landing as lightly as a bird... and there he was, still surprised.

Farion liked to occupy his mind with trying to figure out how the little one did it. It kept his mind off of Veyline. That darned woman wouldn't leave his thoughts.

He was trying very hard not to think about the way the wind played with Vey's silken shirt when an arrow embedded itself in a tree next to him.

Orina was there the next instant with a cry of, "Goblins, lots of them."

Farion smiled.

Finally a good fight. This was what he'd been waiting for: a chance to show the others, Raithan in particular, just how useful he and Storm could be.

Farion had been ranging to the north of the general party, in front and to their left, and immediately turned Storm to race back to them. He assured himself that he wasn't fleeing the enemy, he was warning the party. He hadn't even caught a glimpse of the gray-skinned humanoids, but Orina had known they were coming and they'd gotten the drop on him with an arrow that could have taken him out of the fight early on.

He had to start paying more attention.

The trees here were mostly birch and alder, slender and tall, with lots of room between them, so Storm could gallop full out and easily move around them. It didn't take long for him to reach the party, but Orina was already there. As much as that surprised him, he had no time to ponder it. There were goblins charging in behind him, and the battle was about to be joined. He turned Storm in a tight circle to face them as the rest of the party drew up.

He wasn't going to be able to charge, not yet anyway. The others would be readying their ranged weapons, and getting out into their line of fire would only hinder them. So his newly made lance wouldn't be much use. Instead, he drew his broadsword—the long, thick dual-sided blade good for hacking at things from horseback—off his back.

Then the goblins were there, charging through the trees. Their line stretched as far as the eye could see in either direction, a gray wave crashing through the forest, all teeth and claws and fury.

Farion steeled himself. This wasn't going to be easy, but he still wore a determined grin. Now was his time to shine.

Goblins were no easy foe: they were ferocious, battle-hardened, war-crazed creatures, with sharp claws, razor teeth, and a lust for death in their eyes. Their form, as always, made his skin crawl: ashen-gray skin, blunt faces, bald heads, long, pointed ears, and bodies the size of a man but bulky with hardened muscle and bones like iron.

But he'd faced them before and come out victorious. The fact that there were more this time simply meant he'd have more to be victorious over... hopefully.

Arrow shafts started sprouting from goblins in the lead as Hana and Orina went to work with their bows. Iron balls the size of large oranges flew as well, with frightening speed and accuracy, dropping goblins with a caved in chest or head. Farion still marveled at that, even after a few fights with the big Avdalander. It turned out that big, lumpy bag Alred carried was full of iron balls he used as his ranged weapon with devastating effect. Farion wondered if the big man would have the time to wander around the battle and pick them up as he usually did after this fight, or if they'd be fleeing.

A great gout of fire and force erupted amidst the abominations, throwing goblins and trees alike in all directions. That was new. Farion spared a quick glance away from the charging horde to see Vey, her right hand outstretched and slightly aglow, concentrating on that spot. Now that was some nice magic. Maybe they could survive this assault. He didn't have any more time to wonder, as goblins swarmed over him.

He let out a wild war cry and swung his sword.

This was what he was trained for. With precision and strength, he swung his blade from side to side, wounding and killing goblins as they drew close. Bones cracked. Goblins screamed in pain and fury around him, their foul smell cloying in his nose. He rode with his knees and maintained perfect balance even as Storm reared or kicked back to carry on his own fight against the foul creatures. They were a team, horse and rider, fighting as one. After what seemed like only a short while, the flow of goblins stopped.

Farion and Storm were both breathing hard, and the Lorestin took a moment to gauge the fight around him. There was a pile of goblins around him on all sides, dozens, the odor of death and blood strong. The rest of the party seemed to have fared well and were in the process of finishing off the rest of the horde. Raithan was a vision of precision and death. He was said to be a swordmaster of the highest level. He moved with grace and skill through form after killing form, his blade almost unseen, his bracer-shield always in the way of an enemy attack.

Alred was the complete opposite, chaos incarnate, but just as deadly. Roaring like some savage beast, he spun his great axe around him with ease, lopping off heads or slicing goblins in two. There seemed to be no pattern to his attack, but he was strong enough to move that big blade fast enough that it didn't matter. Veyline was a dervish. Her two long, slender blades were awash in blue flames and dazzled the enemy around her as she laid them to waste in a dance of death. Orina was nowhere to be seen, but her arrows still rained down upon the now fleeing goblins that shrieked as they ran. Krin Hana had her back to a tree and a pile of dead around her, and she also now picked off the retreating goblins. Li Tan used staff and fist to toss, mislead, and finish his foes in what seemed like one winding, weaving movement, so fluid and pure. Even from here, Farion could hear the grunts and cries of the goblins as the Tianese man finished the last of them. Jiska still battled three of the creatures, keeping them at bay with the lightning attacks of her Kirisan, but looked tired. She had had the late watch last night.

Farion spurred Storm over to her aid, crying out and cutting down one of the foes, which gave her the opening she needed to take the other two. She was breathing hard and leaning on her weapon as she gave him a thankful nod. He smiled and returned the nod.

Smoke from Vey's "firebombs" drifted over the impromptu battlefield, acrid and thick. There was only the distant sound of retreating goblins and the heavy breaths of his comrades as they too surveyed the damage.

A horn sounded, followed by a guttural shout.

Orina's voice, high and clear and seemingly all around them, called out, "More! Another wave!"

Well blazes, how many of these things were out there?

In the distance, the next wave of gray-skinned goblins charged through the trees like a flood. Vey sent another blast of magic, throwing goblins and trees alike as if they were ants and twigs, but even as she did, Farion heard her call out, "I can't do much more of those."

Something hardened within Farion at those words. Some voice that sounded suspiciously like his but harder, tougher, somewhere in the back of his mind muttered, "Blast it all!"

He rode over to where he'd rested his long lance against a tree and took it up, moving his sword to his off hand. Then he spun Storm and charged into the oncoming wave of enemies with another wordless war cry.

He sped past gray shapes, all slashing with their heavy swords and axes, or even raking with their razor claws. His lance caught one with a glancing blow and then skewered two more, pinning them to a tree, before he gave the weapon up and resumed his sword work. Farion's fury consumed him as he lost himself in slash after slash of his broadsword. With the force of his strong arms and a charging warhorse behind it, the blade was lethal.

He knew he couldn't deflect all their blows, and he didn't. He could feel pain, but it was distant, almost as if it was happening to someone else.

His rage carried him through the goblin line and past it, but it wouldn't let him rest. He turned Storm sharply to the left and charged along the back of the goblin line cutting them down like a farmer would shafts of wheat.

But calls of warning down the line meant soon he was facing warriors prepared for him, turned from their charge to face him. He found himself in a clump of them and couldn't charge through as there was a cluster of trees before him. They had chosen their ambush well.

Farion laid into the goblins around him, but he'd lost the advantage of his charge and there were far too many swarming in on him. Storm reared and bucked trying to free himself and his rider, but very quickly there was no room to do either.

With a shriek of glee, spittle flying from razor-teeth, a goblin sunk its claws into Farion's right leg and pulled hard, wrenching him from the saddle. But, another on the opposite side had the same idea and jerked him back, leaving him tilted, awkward, with pain shooting through both legs. Some blade slammed into his side and bit through his armor into flesh. He cried out.

Suddenly the goblins pulling on his legs stopped. He was left without counterweights and almost fell from the saddle, but his years of training and riding took over as he gripped the pommel and hauled himself back into his seat.

Now righted, he hacked at one of his assailants. He saw in passing the goblin that had held his leg on the left sinking down under the trampling feet of his brethren with a brightly fletched arrow in his neck.

"Need a hand?" a high-pitched voice called as more arrows seemed to sprout from goblins around him.

Orina.

He couldn't see her, but knowing her, she'd be in the trees somewhere around him. She took out enough of the ones closest to him that he was able to rear Storm and turn around as he did landing on a couple goblins and making himself a way out.

"Much obliged!" he called and then spurred Storm out of the swarm of claws and malice. In an instant he was free and riding hard away from the battle line to give himself some room.

Then miraculously Orina was running beside him, seemingly as fleet-of-foot as Storm, her little legs churning hard.

"This way," she called and indicated with her bow. "The others are retreating to safety this way!"

Farion had trouble believing there was anywhere that was safe in the woods at the moment, but he followed the quick little elf. She sprinted with ease, leading him winding through the trees to a denser section of forest.

"Trust me!" she said before turning suddenly and plunging headlong into what seemed to be a thick tangle of bushes. There was no way she should have been able to get through there, let alone he and his larger mount, but she had said to trust her. Luckily Storm was well trained and trusted his master. The horse hardly balked at being led directly into a thicket.

Yet it wasn't a thicket. Where branches, thorns, and leaves should have been was... nothing. It was an illusion and on the other side stood a great expanse of forest with scattered trees and streaming sunlight. A large brook even burbled out of a clump of rocks and flowed through the area. Orina was standing, waiting for him, and he came to a quick halt.

He wanted to ask what this place was, but with the sudden relief of safety and his adrenaline waning, he simply fainted.

4

"We must move on."

Farion felt as if he'd been floating in darkness for some time and he liked it there: warm, painless, and empty. He didn't recall what had happened prior to being in this place except for the deafening noise, ghastly images of death, and searing pain. So he didn't really want to leave. Yet for some time he'd been hearing voices on the fringes of his oblivion, and now this forceful statement had intruded on his reverie.

He had the impression he knew the speaker, someone forceful who intimidated him, but no name or image came to him in his place.

Another voice spoke, and he got the feeling these two voices had been arguing nearby for some time. "These people are not ready to travel, father." That last word seemed hard for the speaker to say as if she didn't want to admit the other was related to her.

"Have your people make them ready; we need to move. We've been here far too long already."

"It's only been three days. You can afford that and a little longer if it means your people are ready to face what's ahead." There seemed to be definite emphasis placed by both of them on *your people*.

"I knew coming here would be a mistake."

"Coming here was the only thing that saved you from dying, father." This time, the word *father* seemed to have a certain spite and vehemence behind it. "What is it with you humans and unrelenting arrogance?"

"Perhaps it's because we choose to act instead of hide! Maybe we've earned it!"

Now both of them were yelling into Farion's dark, warm place, and it wasn't all that comforting anymore.

"And you wonder why I can't stand to join you in your world."

"Shut up, both of you!" This was a new voice. One he knew well. After a moment of silence, Farion realized it had been his.

He opened his eyes.

Light flooded into his warm, dark place as reality came back to him.

He was outside, looking up through the dappling of leaves and branches at a blue sky. Raithan and Orina were close by, as the names associated with the voices he'd been hearing came to him. He was warm and comfortable, but it was difficult to move. Looking down at his body, which seemed easy to do as his head was slightly raised, he could see he was covered in a blanket woven of leaves and tucked tightly into... a hole in the ground. It looked as if someone had dug a shallow trench that would fit him perfectly. It didn't feel like hard soil he was lying on; it felt more like the earth was embracing him in soft warmth. He was without pain.

His current comfort clashed with his memory of the recent battle and the wounds he'd taken. It occurred to him however, that he had no idea how long he'd been unconscious. Perhaps the battle was not so recent anymore.

Orina was at his side a moment later with some muttered comment to Raithan about talking later.

"How are you feeling?" she asked quietly.

He assessed his condition. "Quite well, surprisingly."

"Good." Her tiny lips spread into a smile which quickly faded into a scowl. "And don't ever think of charging off like that again." Under her breath with a shake of her head, she murmured, "Stupid humans." At that moment, he couldn't blame her for the sentiment. It had been a bit foolhardy of him to run off like that and get himself into a situation he probably wouldn't have survived without her help. He grimaced and nodded sheepishly.

"Are we safe here? Are the goblins still about?"

She shook her head. "This is an elfin glade; no goblin will enter here. You're safe."

He nodded, relaxing with a sigh. "Is everyone else doing well?" he asked.

The scowl turned into a frown, and she shook her head. "No."

"Who...?" He wanted to ask specifically about one in particular but couldn't bring himself to admit it out loud.

"Jiska got the worst. She's alive and will heal, but it will take a while. Alred was pretty badly beaten up too, but apparently it takes a lot more than that to stop an Avdalander." She grinned. "I think half of his injuries came from Hana. The big man scooped her up as he fled—said he could run faster. She didn't take kindly to such treatment. Hana herself took some wounds, one serious, but she'll never admit it. Instead she complains about her bow, lost in the fray." That would be a huge loss for the Mahali archer. "Li Tan seems quite exceptional at avoiding damage, though even he took some light wounds. Raithan is fine, though he should still be resting. He took a nasty wound to the head, even if it wasn't deep." She stopped and harrumphed a sigh, and then looked back at him. "Where was I?"

Only at the most important part!

Her smile came back in a flash at his look. "Oh yes, I did forget someone, didn't I?" She paused for a moment before going on. "Storm is fine and healing well despite the hell you rode him through. His barding protected him from the worst of it, and he's resting at the moment."

Storm! Not the one he'd been thinking of!

But now that he thought of it, how could he forget about his mount, the one companion who had been with him the longest? It was good to know Storm was well.

"And?"

"And? Oh, Veyline, did I not mention her?" There was a definite glimpse of mischief in those large eyes.

No!

"I don't believe so."

"She's fine. Her magic protected her for the most part and helped to cover our retreat." An odd look came over the small elf's face. "She's an odd one for you humans. Her magic is strong."

Farion let out a long breath he hadn't known he was holding.

After a moment, he thought of something else. "Thank you, Orina, for..."

She smiled that wide grin with her small mouth. "Just don't make me save you again."

"Deal." On to other things. "How exactly do I get out of this... bed?"

"The Healing Bed will release you when you're ready."

"I feel ready."

"Indeed you look ready. Why don't you enjoy the view of the branches above and wait a little. I'm sure it will release you soon."

"Soon? How long have I been here? Did you say something about three days?"

"I did, but our healing magic is slow, if thorough. You'll be fine when the bed decides to release you."

"Is there nothing you can do?"

He didn't think it was possible for that tiny grin to get any bigger, but it did. "Oh, of course," she said with a nod, and then got up with a quick spin and strode away.

Farion could see how she might infuriate her father.

He tried to relax, and now that all was quiet around

him it was easier. Even his thoughts of a certain mageblade faded, knowing she was safe.

He must have dozed, for he started awake again sometime later. The sky was darker and evening was upon him. It was only when he raised a hand to brush over his face that he realized he could raise his hands at all. The blanket of leaves was gone—now a light mulch of brown dust covered him—and he was capable of moving as he wished.

It appeared he'd been put in naked, but with a quick scan of the area, he found a pile of clothes set next to his earthen bed. He rose and dressed. A search of the wider area revealed a fire in the distance with a couple forms around it—one of which was Alred; he was hard to miss.

He made his way over.

As he drew near, he saw the forms of Raithan and Hana also sitting near the flames. All of them had steaming bowls of something in front of them which gave off a heady scent that was quite appetizing.

Farion's stomach rumbled. Suddenly he felt as if he hadn't eaten in days, which... he hadn't. He was completely empty and starving.

"Any left?" he asked as he stepped into the firelight and plopped himself down on the ground.

Raithan pointed to a pot next to the flames. "Food's there. Good to see you're up; means we can leave soon. Next time don't get hurt." A man of few words.

Farion opened his mouth, some biting comment on his lips, but another rumble from his stomach stopped him.

Food first, then argument.

He leaned in and grabbed a wooden bowl that sat next

to the steaming pot and ladled himself out a generous helping of what looked to be stew. With no utensils in sight, he shrugged and tilted the bowl to his mouth, taking in what he could. It was hot but not scalding and the broth was delicious. There were chunks of various consistencies, some like boiled potato, some like cooked cabbage, some like peas, and some like apples, but for nothing could he recognize the flavor. It was an odd concoction, mostly because the flavors of whatever was in it were completely new to him.

"What's in this?" he asked around mouthfuls.

"Don't know, but it's delicious," Alred said, going back for more.

Hana finished another sip, talking around her food. "The elves made it. They won't tell us what's in it."

Farion downed another mouthful. Then, something occurred to him.

"Elves? As in more than the one we already have?"

"As in a whole community, yes." This from Raithan, who said no more.

Farion shrugged and turned his attention back to eating.

The fire crackled and snapped, the only sound for a while as Farion and Alred helped themselves to more of the stew.

"Did you just wake up, too?" Farion asked the big Avda-lander, noticing his appetite.

"No, I've been up since yesterday, just hungry."

"Always hungry is more like it," Hana said in a muttered whisper.

"Need energy," Alred replied. "So I can save you again next time." He grinned.

Hana glared at him. "I did not—" She stopped herself and drew in a long breath. "I'm going to bed." She rose and disappeared into the darkness.

"Where do we sleep now?" Farion asked, not that he was tired.

"Under whatever tree you woke up, in the same hole," Alred said between mouthfuls. "There should be blankets waiting for you when you go back. Real blankets." That answered that question but brought up another.

"Where are our hosts? The elves? I'm assuming this is their glade."

"Yes, one of many," Raithan replied. "As for where, they prefer their own company to that of humans. You may see them here or there about, but they like to keep to themselves, secret and distant. It's how they are. I've given up trying to understand them." There was an edge to his voice which Farion thought he understood after the overheard conversation this afternoon.

He wanted desperately to ask how in the blazes of all the hells Raithan had an elf for a daughter. As far as he could tell, she didn't seem any bit human and considered herself to be an elf. So how she came to be his daughter was a mystery. Not that he would ever ask Raithan directly. He was sure the general wouldn't be very forthcoming on the subject.

Raithan excused himself to bed a short while later, and Farion turned to Alred for answers.

"Any idea where Vey and Li Tan are?"

"Bed," was the reply. "Went to sleep early. Raithan was hoping you'd be up today and was expecting to leave tomorrow."

Farion had sated his not inconsiderable hunger, but Alred was still eating. In the Avdalander's defense, there was a lot of him to feed, and this was the best food they'd had in weeks. He watched the big man for a moment, uncertain what to say, uncertain if anything needed to be said. After so long together Farion still marveled at Alred's size, easily over seven feet tall and built like a bear. He didn't have the corded muscles that Raithan had, but he sure had a hell of a lot more: a chest that could rival Storm in width and was nearly as thick through the body as Farion was wide. He had arms like hams, legs like tree trunks, and hands so big they looked like they could grip Farion's head easily, and crush it just as easily. If it wasn't for the jovial grin the massive man wore and the twinkle of mirth in his blue eyes, Farion would have been terrified of him.

"Are all Avdalanders as large as you?"

Alred used a thick finger to spoon out the last of the stew from his bowl and grinned. "I'm half Hallyn."

"Ah." Farion nodded. The Hallyn were a race of "giants" who lived in the mountains around Avdaland. Until today, Farion had considered the stories of Hallyn giants a myth. He had found it hard to believe men could be so big. Now he was having second thoughts about that notion.

Alred tossed the bowl away and sighed a long, heavy breath. "Done." He rose, excusing himself.

Farion sat for a moment, considering his options. He could go back to bed, but he wasn't feeling particularly tired, so he left the fire to wander the glade for a bit. It was full night now, with only a hint of lighter sky in the west. His eyes adjusted quickly to the dark once he was away from the fire. He took a moment to admire the stars above, finely shattered crystal on black velvet. There was no moon tonight, or it had yet to rise, so the stars were clear. He found his favorite constellation, *The Wild Mare*, and smiled. He didn't know why horses comforted him so much. He supposed it was because he'd been around them all his life.

His family bred horses, had done so for thousands of years, even before the Great Journey had brought the seven nations to this new world. They had it down to an art, and their stock was the highest quality in all of Lorest. Farion, as the first son, had Storm, the best of the best.

He wandered around his sleeping area and found the big stallion sleeping peacefully. Tall, strong, fast, and quite a bit more intelligent than your average horse, Storm was a gray stallion, mottled in coloring, like the thunderclouds he was named after. His temperament most of the time belied his name, but get him into battle and he was everything his name implied, dangerous and deadly.

He knelt next to the stallion, stroking his gray coat. Storm lifted his large head and nuzzled into Farion's shoulder.

"Hey, partner, how are you doing?"

Storm whinnied softly and then set his head back down, resting peacefully.

Farion laughed. "Don't want to be disturbed, huh?"

After a little more petting, with Storm breathing easily in sleep, Farion rose and wandered some more.

Again, he had no set destination, and yet again he was pleased when he found where Veyline was sleeping. He didn't get too close. It felt awkward, wrong to be watching her sleep. True, they'd been falling asleep near each other for the past two weeks, but this was different.

His heart ached as he gazed upon her. As odd as it felt to watch her, the thought of curling up next to her seemed natural if she ever asked it of him he'd certainly agree. He could ask her, of course. He was a handsome lord of a high noble family. He'd had his fair share of women, some who'd come to him without having been approached.

Vey was different. He couldn't put his finger on why exactly. Gods, how she befuddled him! Half the time he wasn't sure if he wanted to kiss her or shake her. The other half he just wanted to kiss her. He had approached her several times with some witty comment in his head about them sharing a bedroll, but each time the offer died on his lips. He just wasn't quite sure what he'd do if she said no. The thought of her turning him down caused his gut to clench, his heart to tighten.

"For one who wields such great power, she is quite peaceful when she sleeps."

Farion nearly jumped at the whispered voice next to him. It was Orina, standing quietly next to him. That was how she got you, appearing where and when you least expected it.

He took a moment to calm himself before replying.

"Yes, she is."

They stood there, side by side, for a moment, looking at the mageblade.

"I won't tell her how you feel," Orina said quietly.

"What do you mean?"

"I won't say anything about your feelings for her. I'll leave that to you."

"What feelings? She's a companion on a dangerous quest, that's all." Even as he said the words, he knew they were hollow.

"Really?"

"No."

"I thought so."

"Were you... reading my mind?" Orina had a strange way of always knowing what he was up to, even if he wasn't sure himself.

"What? No." Orina looked up at him with a strange expression. "You humans are confusing. It's been obvious to me for some time that you like her."

"Oh." Farion decided to change the topic, taking the offered opportunity. "You keep saying 'you humans,' but Raithan is your father. Are you not part human, too?"

She sighed deeply. "Yes."

He thought she would say no more than that, but after a moment, she went on. "I was raised with the elves by my mother. I grew up learning their ways. It was all I knew until only just a few years ago when I was told my father wasn't an elf. I was curious and went to see him. I found his world... your world, strange. He thought I'd come and live with him, but I couldn't. I ran away. I wished only to be free. I wandered the Everrun for some time after that. It was during my wanderings, along the Eastern edge of the forest, that I came upon the goblin hordes and the goblin king. I returned to the elves and warned them, but they weren't worried. Goblins never find our glades, but they do ravage human lands, and I felt compelled to tell my father of the threat."

Farion listened quietly and nodded along the way. The tale made sense, though how Raithan had gotten involved with an elfin woman to begin with was a mystery.

Orina let out a long breath. "I'm young still, even by human standards, but the elves teach that life is sacred and not to be wasted. Don't waste yours, Farion. Follow your feelings. You may not have much life left."

Farion sighed and wondered at the wisdom this little one possessed. He looked down at her only to find she'd disappeared yet again. He gave a soft chuckle and walked away. Perhaps he could sleep a little this night.

5

"**B**ut it's one of the most effective weapons we have! Especially against any large groups we face." Vey's voice was raised and Farion could understand why. Orina had just told the mageblade she couldn't use her 'fiery explosion' spell in the forest again.

It was early the next morning, the sun a few spans above the horizon. They had all gathered for a breakfast at the same fire pit as the night before to eat and talk about the remainder of their journey. The only member of the party not present was Jiska, still out cold and recovering in her little cocoon. The decision had been made to move on without the Numorian. According to the elves she would need several more days to heal fully. The rest of them were healed and could travel. She'd be safe here. It wasn't an easy decision, but Raithan's need to move had overcome any objections. They'd head out before noon that day. The final details were being worked out at the moment.

Vey was standing with hands on curvy hips, staring down at the elf. Orina sat, eyes passive, calm in her relentlessness. "Yes, I understand, but you must also understand that we elves tend and respect the forest, as we do with all life. Even though your spell destroys many of the enemy it also destroys the forest just as equally and we feel such losses deeply."

Veyline sighed heavily.

They'd been arguing this point for some time and Veyline was the last holdout. Others had argued her side. Farion himself had only just conceded the point. The quiet, stoic argument of the elf wore them all down. Now they just accepted that they were in someone else's "house" and had to live by their rules. It looked like Vey was just about to come to the same conclusion.

She tried one last time. "If we face another force like the one that drove us in here and there isn't an elfin glade to run to, this mission will be over before it even reaches the Eastern Mountains. We need an offensive weapon."

"You're correct," Orina said calmly. "If we face such a force as before and there is no glade to run to, we're all dead. What we need instead is stealth. We'll need to move carefully from now on and avoid such forces before they get to us. The last attack was my fault. I hadn't known goblins had such a strong sense of smell. We were upwind of them and they knew we were around long before we knew they were. Now that I know that, I can counter it. That's how we must proceed."

"Orina is right," was Raithan's response. "The whole

point of a force our size is to move quickly and quietly and not be noticed."

Farion had to admit that he grudgingly agreed with Raithan despite wanting Veyline to be able to win this fight somehow.

Vey sighed again and after a moment nodded slowly, throwing hands out to her side in surrender and sitting. "All right."

"However," Orina said with a slow grin spreading on her face, "once we're free of the forest, if we're noticed and attacked by any hordes of goblins, feel free to use any and all of your most powerful spells including that one. The rocks of the mountains care little for such damage."

Vey returned the smile. "Noted."

They eventually agreed that a mixture of Veyline's magic and Orina's forest lore would be used to keep them from being noticed by more goblins, which elfin scouts reported were thick in the woods they would have to travel from now on. They would travel by day since goblins possessed incredible senses, particularly scent and night vision, which would give the enemy the advantage during darker hours. When all was set, they gathered their equipment and came together again near one of the false thickets that surrounded the glade.

Hana was grinning from ear to ear and held a new bow in her hand. She held it up to show the others. "An elfin bow," she said. "It's smaller than mine, but I've tested it, and it's a superb weapon. Perhaps even better than mine was."

"The elves have much experience with such weapons," Orina said cryptically.

Once they'd all arrived, Orina spread a viscous mixture on them and their equipment, meant to foul the goblin's ability to scent them out. It didn't smell particularly bad, but it was pungent and made Farion feel like he needed to bathe, despite having done so that morning. Storm didn't seem to mind it though.

They left the elfin glade by midafternoon and traveled in a tight group, with Farion walking Storm and staying with the others. They needed to remain close. Veyline cast an obscuring field around them, which rendered them undetectable by sight or hearing. With Orina's poultice obscuring their scent, their ruse was complete. It was a tense afternoon as they spotted several goblin patrols slinking through the woods. It seemed their deception was working, as none of the goblins noticed them.

Orina, always able to be obscure on her own, scouted their path ahead and led them around any large parties of goblins.

Their first snag came that night as they made camp. Veyline placed an obscuring spell around the area for the night and promptly collapsed. Farion ran to her, as did Hana and Li Tan. She was conscious and as they got to her she sat up slowly, unsteady.

"That worked me harder than I thought it would," she said, her voice hoarse. Hana brought out some water and let her drink. "Thank you." Veyline's eyes were unfocused, and she looked like she'd been working herself to the bone and not slept in days. Still, she managed a faint smile but then seemed to drift off for a moment. She hadn't been standing, only sitting, but she still fell back. Farion caught her as her arms, which had been supporting her went limp. She came around again quickly. "Did I faint again?"

Farion nodded.

"This isn't good." Vey sighed deeply. "Get me some food and more water and gather the others. We need to talk."

They did as told, and once Veyline had had something to eat and drunk nearly two full water skins, she seemed a bit more stable. The other companions finished setting up the small camp, having to remain inside the boundaries of Vey's obscuring field. Also, since a fire would create a scent for the goblins to track, they lit none. They'd have no light and a cold supper. They gathered around Veyline where she lay propped up on Farion's saddlebags, night deepening around them. She laid out the bad news.

"I can't keep this up. I didn't think my shield would drain me in this way, but then I've never used it to conceal such a large area for so long. Usually I hide in a much smaller version, and only for a short period of time. I won't be able to keep it up all day tomorrow."

"You could ride Storm—that would keep you from any physical exertion," Farion suggested.

She smiled. "I appreciate the sentiment but it won't help. Even not walking, the field won't last all day. It's just too big for too long."

"Will it last the night?" Raithan asked, concerned.

She nodded. "The one in place now is no strain on me.

If it's not moving, I can secure it in one spot and release the spell. It will last almost indefinitely, or until I dispel it."

"Such is the way with elfin magic, also," Orina said.

Farion was a little surprised to hear this. "Do you have magic, too? Is that how you keep yourself so well hidden? Can you do the same spell and help her out?"

Orina smiled. "I wish I could, but no. I never studied magic, as some elves do, but in a way you're correct. There are some things all elves can do naturally that are similar to magic, but I can't help others with it. It would be like you trying to breathe for me; it's just... something I can do naturally."

"Ah."

"So what do we do?" came the stiffly accented voice of Li Tan.

"We can stay here until she's fully rested," Alred suggested.

"No," Raithan said. "We must move quickly; time is short. We can't afford to rest three days for every day of travel."

"Then what can we do?" Hana asked in her singsong voice.

"Be more careful," Orina said evenly.

"How do you mean?" Raithan asked.

"If we move slower—" She raised a hand to stop Raithan's instant rebuttal to those words. "If we move slower, I can scout ahead and pick a path for us where goblins are not. Their sense of smell seems to be their primary early warning that enemies are about. We have already countered that. If we get into a situation where we're outflanked then Veyline can use her field to hide you all as you move or even stay in one spot until the trouble has passed. We'll lose time, yes, but we'll get there all in one piece, and all with relative strength. Face it, Father, with this many goblins around, we simply can't keep the pace you want to keep. We need to be more careful."

Raithan's look could have cut steel, but Orina seemed impervious. Raithan drew in a long breath then rose suddenly and began pacing. His eyes seemed to search for some hidden answer amongst the trees around them. Finally he stopped, turning to Veyline.

"How long do you think you can keep up your shield without tiring while we move?"

"I honestly don't know. I'd guess for an hour at most, and after that, I may need to ride Storm to rest for a bit."

Farion could tell that wasn't the answer Raithan wanted to hear. "Then it would appear we'll do this my daughter's way." With that, he rose and strode the two steps to his bedroll. When he left, so too did the tension they all felt. It was as if they all sighed at once.

"It's settled then," Farion said with a nod.

The rest of them ate a cold meal in a tight circle.

Alred grumbled about the lack of food compared to the sumptuous meals they'd had with the elves. Hana slapped his arm and told him to be grateful for what he had.

"I remember a time much like this," Li Tan said starting another of his usually amusing stories. "I was a young man and had just mastered Snake Style. I was looking for a master to teach me Heron Style, as I thought I would be a good student for it. There was a famine at that time. Three years of drought meant little food for the peasants. Many died." This story was definitely not as humorous as most. "I was in the far south of Tian, Yu-Han prefecture, on a small river just outside of a village called Sen-Chi. I'd found some..." he searched for the word for some time, "I believe you call them cattails and was boiling the stalk and the root to eat. One of the villagers must have noticed my small fire and came to me, asking what I was cooking. When I told him, he looked amazed. 'You can eat those?' he asked. Within ten minutes, the entire village was out and the whole patch of the cattails had been harvested. They were simple folk—miners, I believe—and they hadn't known they had a store of food so close by. The looks on their faces as they ate... they were so grateful for even that small meal. I'll never forget that." He chuckled softly to himself.

"I wish I had some boiled cattails," Alred mumbled.

Hana slapped his arm again.

They all laughed.

Slowly they dispersed to their respective bedrolls.

Orina caught Farion's eyes as she heading to bed. She nodded toward Veyline, mouthing *"tell her."*

Farion grimaced. His stomach churned at the thought. Though he did stay with Veyline a moment longer after the others had left.

He opened his mouth to say something... anything about how he felt, but all that came out was, "Vey, I... was wondering if there's anything else you need?"

Vey got an odd look in her eyes as she looked deeply into his. "No, a good sleep is all I need now."

Farion nodded and was about to rise when one of Veyline's hands found his and gave it a squeeze. "Thank you for asking, though."

He smiled, filled with a warm, unfamiliar sensation. "Any time."

6

After that, the going was slow but steady. They fell into a tight rhythm of vigilant stalking through the forest, waiting at predefined points for Orina's signal to proceed and using Vey's shield sparingly to get them through the worst of the goblin infestation. At night, Veyline would put up a static shield to keep them hidden and every morning Orina would come with more of her poultice to keep them smelling like... nature. In this manner, they made their way through the rest of the Everrun Forest. It took them an extra week, but they made the forest edge without incident.

It was getting into high summer now, and the days were hot and long.

They proceeded with extreme caution now that they were out from the cover of the forest and onto the foothills of the Eastern Mountains. They kept as much as they could to valleys and canyons, careful to heed Orina's word on when to hide, when to move, and how to move.

Late on the second day out from the forest they were walking beside a shallow creek in the hollow between two rounded hills when Orina came sprinting over one of the hills, calling for Vey to put her shield up. Vey did so. A moment later Orina was within it. Only a heartbeat after that a gray-skinned wave of goblins came marching over the hill where Orina had been.

All the companions seemed to sense the problem at the same time.

"Vey, will this field...?"

"No, we need to move."

"Where to? There's nothing out here," Hana breathed.

"There." Raithan pointed to a small clump of three trees. "They'll have to go around those."

They quickly made their way to the trees and hid in, around, and behind them as best they could. The problem wasn't being seen—the shield would protect from that. The problem was being run over! The goblins were so thick, so numerous, and marching in such a pack, that had they remained out in the open the creatures would have marched right through Veyline's shield. Hopefully they'd go around this clump of trees and in doing so go around the group.

The first thing Farion noticed as the goblins drew near was the discipline and order of the group. Most of the goblins they'd faced so far had been rather wild and unorganized. The one band he'd encountered in Lorest had had a leader and followed orders, but this was different. More than just organized, these goblins were regimented, marching in tight formation... trained. The second thing he noticed was their armor. They all wore uniform armor: long chain shirt, breastplate, bracers, and greaves. The third thing was the sheer number of them. The force they'd fought by the elfin glade had been a few hundred. This was more like a few thousand, line after long line, and they just kept coming. The last thing was their leader, mounted on what appeared to be a giant wolf, riding behind the lines in heavy armor, carrying a massive sword. He had to be half-again as big as the average goblin and looked twice as tough and mean.

"Hobgoblin," Orina whispered in his ear. "On a warg no less. Rare."

He said nothing in return, his heart sinking more and more with each passing line of the beady-eyed creatures. A force of so many well-trained and provisioned warriors would be tough to defeat. This one army would prove a challenge for any army of the Seven Kingdoms, though it would be defeated eventually. If there were many more like this though... the kingdoms of the East would be in for a war like none they'd ever known.

The massive horde was still passing around their clump of trees, coming down off the hill. The leader paused at the top of the hill to watch his troops.

A grunt, soft but still audible over the marching horde, issued somewhere behind Farion.

He turned quickly to see Alred with one of the goblins in a crushing bear hug, a huge hand over the thing's mouth. With a rather small, yet quick movement the large Avdalander snapped the creature's head to the side and it went limp. They all remained perfectly quiet despite knowing that Vey's shield blocked out sound, until the rest of the horde had passed, and even the leader had ridden by.

Once the coast was clear, Farion dared to breathe again. "What happened?" he whispered, motioning to the goblin who Alred had let slip to the ground.

Li Tan answered, "One of them got too close, stepped into the field, and saw us. Alred was ready. For one so big, he moves with amazing speed."

"I thank all possible gods every day that he's on our side," Farion said in awe.

"Agreed," was the response from the short Tianese. "I've never met a man I couldn't beat with my skill in the five styles. He's the first where I have doubts." It seemed a rather strong boast and yet honest and evenly delivered.

"Good to know," Farion said, realizing that the Tianese man had already sized him up and found him wanting. Not that Farion wanted to fight the man; he wasn't sure he would ever land a blow the way the small man could move.

"Are we clear?" Hana asked, her bow ready. Her eyes searched the hillsides for enemies.

"I'll check. Stay here," Orina said quietly. She pointed at the dead goblin. "And bury him. If other goblins smell him it may alert them to our presence." With that, she was gone up the hill.

"She's right," Raithan said, putting down his pack and removing a small spade. They all took turns digging until they had a hole deep enough for the goblin. They dumped it in and covered it, smoothing the dirt out to mask the grave as best they could. By the time they were done Orina had returned.

Her small face, usually so jovial and sprightly, was clouded and dour, a tight frown on her small lips. Her eyes stared off into the distance, not meeting any of theirs as she spoke.

"There's something you all need to see. Vey, you should keep your shield up, if you can; this won't take too long. Follow me."

She led them along the floor of the valley and through another low pass and then up to the top of a ridge, which they'd been working their way toward all day. It was higher than any of the hills so far. As they reached the top, they could see what Orina had been concerned about.

The other side of the ridge was a sheer drop, so there was no worry that goblins might come over the ridge at them. That wasn't really the problem, though. The issue was the massive number of goblins below.

They overlooked a large valley of lower hills, the other side of which was the rocky side of the Eastern Mountains rising like jagged teeth into the sky. Nearly the entirety of that large, long valley was occupied by goblins. Camps spread over the hills below with cooking fires burning all over the place. To Farion it seemed like an impossible number of goblins. His heart fell.

So many, so well organized... the Seven Kingdoms would stand little chance.

"Over five hundred thousand at a rough count," Raithan said, his voice grave. "Largest army I've ever seen." And there was no doubt that it was an army. This is what would be marching on their lands if they didn't get rid of the goblin king.

"How can you count so many so quickly?" Hana asked, breathless, obviously still awed by the sight before them.

"Easy, I did a rough count of that army that passed us in the trees, rough numbers per line, multiplied by the number of lines. It looked to be roughly ten thousand. I can see similar groupings below, roughly fifty or so."

Made sense.

"How will we ever get past?" Alred asked. It was the first time Farion had heard the big man sound uncertain. "I don't think Vey's shield will get us through that."

"It won't," was Vey's clipped response.

"There." Orina pointed. "That ridge along one end of the valley. We'll be exposed, but there are no camps. If we're careful, perhaps we can make it across."

"That's roughly a day's traveling along an exposed area. I don't like it," Raithan said and then sighed heavily. "But I see no other way."

"We'll move slowly using Vey's shield and stop often to let her rest. It may take a couple of days, but we should remain unseen," Orina suggested. It seemed a good idea to Farion... except for the part where they were wearing out their mage, the one who could hurl fire at large groups of enemies.

"Why don't we move away from here and make camp, and then we can discuss it." This from that very mage.

"Agreed." Raithan nodded and moved away from the ridge. Farion was glad to leave that sight behind.

7

They were a somber crew as they took their meal that evening. They all knew what lay just over the ridge in the next valley. They all knew that their trek ahead would be treacherous. Yet they knew now —after what they had seen that afternoon—more than ever how important their mission was and that they had to continue on. Simply walking away at this point wasn't an option, and they all knew it. Death on the other hand...

Li Tan tried to lighten the mood as they ate, telling several humorous tales about his training. He did manage to get everyone to laugh at his description of a particularly nasty teacher and how he'd finally beaten the man, tripping him into a nearby river.

After that Alred, apparently feeling more like himself, began grumbling about the lack of food. This was a usual supper event despite that the big man usually had twice the portion of the rest of them.

Hana just rolled her eyes. Being the second smallest of the lot of them, it seemed she had little sympathy for him.

"Shouldn't have grown so big in the first place," she muttered.

Li Tan laughed.

"Something tells me he didn't have much choice in the matter," Farion said, grinning.

"Still." The look Hana gave the Avdalander was softer than her words. A faint smile played on her lips.

"You didn't complain last night when all this helped keep you warm," Alred said, motioning with both hands at his ample body.

"And I won't tonight, either."

Alred grinned as a mischievous look crossed Hana's eyes.

Farion just shook his head. The two of them had been pushing their bedrolls closer and closer for several nights now, despite their outward animosity to each other.

Hana and Alred left shortly after, pushing their bedrolls together again. Tonight would be a good night for comfort with a companion.

That thought brought back Orina's words from what seemed like a lifetime ago: *Follow your feelings. You may not have much life left.*

It seemed much more possible now; time seemed very short indeed. Having watched Hana and Alred come together despite their great many differences, perhaps...

He had tried so many times over the last three weeks to talk to Veyline. He'd struck up many conversations with the attractive mageblade in hopes that his feelings would come out somehow as they spoke, but inevitably they didn't and he would fall asleep still aching, still hollow.

Yet the urgency and pressing danger of their current situation somehow made it even harder for him to say anything. He sat there mulling over what to say in his head, trying to figure out how to verbalize exactly what it was he was feeling.

Orina even gave a subtle yet suggestive nod in Veyline's direction while they finished their food, but still he didn't know how to express himself. What made it worse was that he was taking the first watch that night. Even as the others bedded down he sat thinking, trying to make sense of what he felt.

Finally, though uncertain, yet unwilling to go another moment in silence, he rose and made his way over to where Vey lay on her side, her back to him, sleeping. He had to say something. This was his last chance, his only chance. He felt like he would explode if he didn't say something... and felt that his entire world would explode if he did. He laid a hand on her shoulder. He meant to shake her or say her name or something, but his hand simply rested there.

He managed a whisper. "Vey." She didn't stir.

Then it hit him. Perhaps she didn't need to be awake for him to speak. Suddenly the words came in a flood.

He whispered, his voice barely audible, "Vey, I... like you a lot. I think I have since the moment I first saw you. If so then as I got to know you, I've only grown to care for you more and more. You're strong, passionate, mysterious, and playful. Everything I am, well, except for the mysterious part. I don't know what will happen to us in the days to come, but I wanted you to know that I will be there for you, that you are important to me. Even with all this looming over us, I think you're the most important thing in the world to me. I think... I... Oh hell, blast it all! I love you, Vey." Then he remembered he was talking to her slumbering form. "Even if you don't know it." He sighed out a long, heavy breath, nodding to himself with a faint smile. He'd said what he needed to say. He removed his hand from her shoulder, rose, and went back to keeping watch.

He found he was at peace with himself. After he woke Raithan to relieve the watch, he slept well for the few hours that remained to him.

8

They made good time working their way stealthily toward the ridge at the far end of the long valley. Yet the morning of the day they were to cross the ridge trouble arose and it had nothing to do with goblins. That would have been easy for Farion to handle. No, this was much more disturbing.

Farion and Raithan stood toe to toe, glaring at each other, neither willing to yield. Farion met Raithan's icy blue eyes, which were hard and unlikely to melt anytime soon.

"He must stay." Raithan's tone was firm.

"Storm goes where I go." It had been his mantra since they'd risen that morning and Raithan had told him Storm could go no farther.

"I told you from the start that a warhorse would be of little use where we're going. The closer we get to the goblin king's lair, the less likely we are to find any place where Storm will be safe. Here will do."

"But…"

"The legends say the lair of the goblin king is deep within that mountain," Raithan said, pointing to the gray-sided mass that rose high on the other side of the ridge they were looking to start across that day. "How will Storm fair in the caves and crevices as we descend beneath it?"

It was a valid point. Horses in general were unused to being underground, but Storm was well trained. He would do as Farion instructed. Farion told Raithan as much.

"Blazes, man! Can't you see? It just won't work." Raithan's explosion forced Farion back a step.

He could see. He knew Raithan was right, but he'd be damned if he would admit it to Raithan. Infuriated with himself and this man before him he raised a fist to strike… only to have it stopped by a delicate, gloved hand.

"Farion, come with me," Vey said softly beside him. Then to Raithan: "You step away. You're not helping."

Raithan spun and stalked off, muttering something about, "idiot Lorestin knights."

Farion allowed himself to be led by Veyline to the shade of a nearby tree. Orina followed.

"Are you calm?" Vey asked.

"No." Farion was still roiling on the inside, unable to come to terms with this situation.

Vey laid a tender hand on his shoulder. "Calm down." The words echoed and resonated within him, and he felt his heart slow, his anger fade.

"Neat trick," Orina said. "I wish I could do that on father."

Farion breathed a long, deep sigh and hung his head.

"I'm a knight," he said slowly. "What am I without my mount?" And that was what it came down to. He'd fought and lived through some pretty hairy fights so far. He'd held his own amongst these champions, but without Storm—without that advantage—what was he but just another man with a sword.

Veyline put a gloved finger to his chin, lifting his head until his eyes met hers. Soft brown depths shimmered as she held his gaze with compassion. "I guess we'll see, won't we?"

She smiled and he found himself smiling with her. His heart lifted.

For her he could be a knight without a horse. He would show her what he could be. He'd show them all and put Raithan straight on that matter once and for all.

He nodded slowly. "Give me a moment," he said, his voice low, and then he made his way over to Storm.

He spoke to Storm as he would to any other human. The warhorse was smart enough and understood in his own way. He lowered his voice though, so the others wouldn't hear.

"I guess this is it, buddy." He patted Storm on his high shoulder, and the horse turned his head nuzzling Farion's shoulder in return. "I may not make it back from this. Frankly I think I'd have a better chance of making it back if you were coming with me, but apparently that's not going to happen."

Storm whinnied softly.

"I know, I'll miss you, too." Farion embraced Storm's thick neck. "Take care of yourself. You've got enough grazing around here to last you for a while if you don't gorge yourself." Farion then went about making the area Storm-friendly. He took the feedbag of oats and hung it from a tree and then set a bag of apples, of which only a few remained, open on the ground.

"Stay. Guard." Farion gave the commands. The two in conjunction would convey to remain in this general area.

Vey placed a shield around the area to protect Storm, just in case. They hadn't seen any goblins in the area around the ridge. The small copse of trees with the river next to it was secluded in a small bowl of land. With any luck no goblins would wander by. Storm would know enough to hide if he heard anyone coming, and hopefully Orina's paste would keep any stray goblins from smelling him. All in all, the horse would be fine here.

Farion just didn't know if he himself would be fine. Once all was set and his tears—which he made sure none of his companions saw—were shed, he hugged Storm one last time and gave him another pat on the shoulder. "Take care." Then he turned and walked away, not bearing to look back.

He reached the others, unable to look at any of them. "Let's go."

As they set out that morning, they found themselves on the cusp of the ridge fairly quickly. It was in fact part of the same ridge they'd been on a few nights before when they'd seen the goblin armies. It curved around a massive area, creating a bowl in which the armies were sitting. The other side, the northwest end of the bowl, was much more sloped and seemed to be where the majority of the armies were exiting the valley once they were ready to march. They'd been right in the path of any such force two days ago; now they were well out of range of the hundreds of thousands of goblins below. This end of the bowl was a steep rock face for about two hundred feet. It would take skilled or very determined climbers to scale. There shouldn't be any goblins coming at them from that side.

Orina had been scouting ahead and returned to them, the pale skin of her face even more ashen.

"What is it?" Raithan asked.

Orina shook her head slowly. "Not good." She opened her mouth a few times but no words came out. That was very out of character for the little elf. Farion developed a rather uncomfortable feeling in the pit of his stomach watching her. She was a fearless and usually cheery companion, but the way she looked at them all now made Farion uneasy. His apprehension only grew the longer she remained silent. He didn't like this, not at all.

Eventually Orina found the words she'd been searching for, or perhaps trying to avoid. "More goblins. Many more. This is going to be difficult. Go ahead, up to the top of the ridge there and take a look for yourself."

Farion wasn't the first to reach the high point of the ridge. He wasn't sure he wanted to look judging from the reactions of the others.

"By all the gods and ancestors!" came Hana's breathed curse.

Alred just stood there, shaking his head slowly.

"Where could they all come from?" Raithan seemed to be taking it best.

On second thought, Li Tan was taking it the best. He simply walked back from the view smiling that grin of his. "This should be fun," he said. That might have scared Farion the most.

Farion reached the top of the rise and peered down to the south and east.

His breath left him. It was a long moment before he drew a shuddering breath to replace it.

There were two valleys.

The first they had spent the last two days moving around, heading to the high ridge which ran from southwest to northeast at the one end. Yet now that they were on that ridge they could see the second valley, as big as the first, running roughly eastward, with just as many goblins in it.

The worst part was this valley had several ways into and out of it, one of which was up the rise they were about to cross over. The slope of the ridge where it descended into the second valley was not overly steep and depending on how the goblins below chose to exit the valley they could walk right into Farion and his companions. Also, if any goblins below happened to see or smell the party, they could charge up the ridge in a matter of minutes and swarm the allies entirely.

"Blazes," Farion whispered drawing another long, shuddering breath. He turned to the others. "How will we ever get past so many?"

"My shield," Vey said slowly. "It's the only way."

"We've already established you can't keep it up all day long," Farion said, worried for the mageblade.

"Then we'll use it in short spurts and I'll sleep when I need to. We can use a static field while we rest. It just means..."

"We're going to be spending a day or two crossing that ridge," Orina finished.

"Yes," Vey said, nodding.

Raithan grimaced. Farion had to agree with the sentiment.

He breathed a long sigh. "Great."

9

Since Vey's shield would keep them out of sight and Orina's ever-present odor-masking paste would keep them out of "scent" they simply walked across the top of the ridge as quickly as they could.

After a couple of hours, however, it became apparent that it wouldn't be enough.

Veyline staggered and would have fallen if Farion, who had been watching her like a hawk, had not stepped in and caught her. She smiled at him with a nod and righted herself.

She was already looking weary and they still had a long way to go to reach the other side.

By late afternoon Farion was half-carrying the weary mageblade and she whispered to him that she couldn't go on.

He called a halt and with the little strength she had left, Vey put up a static field around them and promptly collapsed into sleep.

So they made camp on the side of a rise overlooking a million or more well-trained and well-organized goblins. None of the group could rest well. Farion finally succumbed to sleep as darkness fell, thankful that tonight wasn't his watch.

He was shaken awake while it was still dark. Hana was on late watch and it looked like she'd woken the others before him, as it was Alred who shook him. He came awake quickly, knowing the situation they were in.

"What is it?" he whispered.

"Goblin patrol heading this way," Alred whispered back.

Farion nodded, rose, and drew his sword from his back. He peered into the darkness and could see the shapes of about a dozen goblins moving across the top of the ridge. They'd be here in about a half hour at their current leisurely pace. Pale light edged the other side of the mountain peaks. It was nearly dawn.

"She won't wake," was the urgent whisper from close by. He looked over to see Hana beside Vey and his heart skipped a beat. He hurried over and knelt beside the prone and unmoving mageblade.

Hana must have seen the concern on his face as she smiled reassuringly. "She's not dead, but her sleep is so deep she won't wake."

He let out a long breath he hadn't known he was holding and nodded. *Thank all the gods for that, at least*, he thought.

"Let her sleep then," he said calmly.

The look in Hana's eyes changed to confusion and she shook her head. "But if she doesn't wake we can't move."

It took a moment before Farion registered the full scope of their problem. They'd be invisible to the goblins as long as that patrol didn't happen to wander into Vey's obscuring field, in which case they might be in trouble. They'd have to silence the entire patrol quickly and hide them before any other goblins noticed. Even then, someone would surely notice the patrol was missing after some time. The only way to avoid them was to have Vey awake and moving around the patrol with her shield up to ensure they weren't discovered. If Vey didn't wake then they had to pray the patrol didn't blunder right into them. Something told Farion their luck wouldn't be that good.

Half an hour later he was certain their luck had run out. Vey was still not awake or responding to attempts to wake her and the patrol was only a short distance away and heading straight for them.

All the companions were ready. The best-case scenario now would be if all of the goblins entered Vey's shield. That way, if they could all be dispatched quickly, the static field would keep any noise from the fight from warning others. If only some entered then the archers would have their job cut out for them. Already both Hana and Orina had two arrows notched in hopes of taking down two targets at once. The rest of them had weapons ready for whatever might happen.

Only three of the goblins entered the obscuring field. Farion didn't even get an attack in. One massive swing of

Alred's axe took down two of them and Raithan got the third. Most of the ladies' arrows hit home, taking down three and wounding another. Li Tan stepped out of the field to finish the wounded one and strike another in the throat, negating its ability to call out. That however, was only eight of the twelve in the patrol. The others were surprised, but only for so long.

Two more went down to arrows before they even had a chance to act, and Li Tan was spinning into the other two as they reacted. The first was drawing a weapon and went down with a nasty kick to the head, snapping its neck. The second had a horn to its mount and was blowing by the time Li Tan reached him. His throat was struck and an arrow took him down a moment later, but it was too late. The horn had sounded, even if only for a second. Its clear, clipped call echoed across the valleys around them, and as dawn broke over the high mountain peaks they could all see activity in the many camps below.

"Now we're burned," Farion said to no one in particular.

"We need to move now!" Raithan said, gathering his equipment.

"Won't it be safer to stay hidden in the shield?" Hana asked.

"Not once they get up here and start looking around. If one of them blunders in here with a thousand more around, I don't think we'll be able to make it out."

She nodded to that and after a moment they were all ready to go. They could only hope that the still dim light of dawn wouldn't be enough for the goblins below to see them run. Without giving it a second thought, Farion scooped up Veyline once his pack was on and Alred took her gear.

They ran out across the ridge, making sure to keep below the peak so no one on either side would be able to see their silhouettes against the new dawn sky.

Farion was glad for the solid sleep of the previous night as he found reserves of strength and endurance he didn't know he had. He was a fit man, strong and lean, but he wasn't used to running for this long—that's what a horse was for. But the others kept going and he'd be damned if he fell behind even if he was carrying extra weight. Alred offered a few times to take Vey, but Farion refused. It made perfect sense to take the big man up on his offer, but Farion didn't want to let her go. Eventually Alred stopped asking.

Full light of day was on them before they'd made it to the cover of the few trees and brush on the mountainside. They'd been noticed, that much was clear. Horns were sounding all across the valley and echoing over the mountains and there was a small horde of goblins charging up the ridge toward them. It was a long way up that ridge, and charging uphill was difficult. It looked like that would slow the goblins down enough that they wouldn't reach the group until the companions were at the mountainside. If that was the case they might have a chance to hide or evade the goblins, as fighting now was almost certainly not a favorable option.

They ran hard and it quickly became clear that they would reach the mountains before the goblins reached them. There were caves there as well as scattered woods and heavy brush. They might just get away and be able to confuse the goblins long enough for Vey to wake up and hide them. Farion had a moment of hope.

A fleeting moment.

With his next breath, he saw several patrols of the gray-skinned creatures coming down the mountainside toward them. The companions were trapped.

They could probably take the patrols if they stopped to fight, but doing so would give the others behind them time to catch up. As far as Farion could see, they had two options, neither of which was great. The first was run headlong into the patrols, fighting quickly so those behind would hopefully not be able to reach them. The second option was to turn to their left and run for as long as they could before the patrols caught them. It would put those coming up the hill directly behind them and help increase distance, but it also meant that the patrols wouldn't reach them as fast, and if that fight took too long, the others would finish them.

Raithan chose to turn to the left and they all picked up speed, exhausted as they were. For a moment it looked like they might have even outmaneuvered the patrols, but it wasn't to be. And it was Farion who was the cause. He was farthest back, and he knew he wouldn't be able to engage an enemy with Vey in his arms. He had to stop, put her down, and draw his sword. For a moment, before the others realized he'd stopped, he was alone facing a few dozen enemies, with thousands more not far behind.

For some reason he smiled.

If this was how he was going to go out, he was going to take as many of them with him as he could and defend Veyline to his dying breath. He let out a great war-cry and widened his stance a little to give himself more stability to meet their charge.

Then Alred was next to him on one side and Li Tan on the other. Three against three thousand—well, it sure beat one against three thousand.

In the single breath of a moment, before the goblins were on them, Alred whispered, "Raithan and the others are going on ahead to try and complete the mission. We're to keep these critters off their back for as long as possible."

Farion smiled. At least his death would have meaning, helping others achieve the mission he'd set out on.

Then the goblins were on them and there was no more time for idle thought.

It was strange fighting static—not moving, not being above the fray on horseback—but battle was battle and he'd trained in non-mounted combat. He'd just never actually been in non-mounted combat.

Parry, strike, slice into another parry, side-step and block, throw off weapon, punch, parry, slice; the flow of combat was endless. Goblins fell before him, but others came in. The three of them moved apart a bit to allow for the swing of their weapons and to block a larger area of goblins from passing them. A spear caught Farion's shoulder guard solidly. The weapon didn't puncture, though his shoulder would have a great bruise no doubt, but it did knock him back half a step, turning him.

For a heartbeat, he could see the body of Veyline lying not far behind him. He turned back to cut the spear in two and skewer its owner, but the damage was done.

That one glimpse of the woman he loved threw his thoughts into chaos. If he died, who would protect her? Would she die while still unconscious? Was that better? Just the thought of her death was too much of a distraction.

A mace slipped past his defenses, bashing him hard in the side of the head. His helm took the brunt of the blow, but pain exploded across his skull. The attacker, too cocky and trying to press his advantage, went down to an instinctive slice by Farion, but that had been lucky.

His vision was blurry. He was dizzy.

He staggered to one side, which saved him from another blow. He blocked what he thought was an attack but found no weapon there; he'd been too slow, and a blade cut into his side... deeply.

He lashed about wildly, feeling his blade bite into goblin as often as not. A blow to the back of his neck staggered and surprised him. He went to one knee, lashing out behind him and feeling the blade sink into something significant, but he was off balance and his blade was at an odd angle. Another blow to the shoulder knocked him to the ground, and he was forced to let go of his sword still stuck in the enemy behind him. Another stab to his back, driving deep; he felt blood rush out with the sword.

He was on his face in the dirt unable to move. The

scent of mud, blood, and sweat was close and cloying. The clash and din of combat rang around him.

He knew the killing stroke would come, just as he knew he'd failed Vey.

He lost all hope as a final blow to the head sent him into eternal darkness.

10

F arion opened his eyes to an intense brightness. His first thought was that he'd passed into the spirit world.

After a moment, within the light he could discern shapes.

Everything was bright and surrounded with a hazy halo, no sharp lines or harsh contours. This must be the spirit world, for nowhere else could such beauty exist. Before him was a mountain spring waterfall, which splashed into a small pool before trickling down the mountainside. The only sound was the rush and burble of water. The waterfall was surrounded by a loose cluster of pine trees. Through those trees filtered a great, blazing light. The sky above was myriad shades from deep blues and purples to blazing oranges and pinks. There was soft grass beneath him and something warm and soft for a pillow under his head. The final clue that he was in the spirit world was the water nymph bathing in the waterfall's shower. She was the most beautiful creature he'd ever seen, with her head thrown back into the stream, dark hair caught by the water. The pale, perfect body could only be the work of the gods. He closed his eyes again capturing that image. Such a sight was too much for mortal eyes and truly he must be dead. He was tired, so very tired. He let himself sink back into the warm darkness of a restful sleep.

Pain woke him later. He wouldn't have thought he'd feel pain as a spirit, but his entire body ached in a continuous throbbing pulse. He opened his eyes to darkness. It was night.

Was there night in the spirit world?

Apparently.

There was some source of light and heat behind him and the crackling of a fire. He rolled over. A process that elicited myriad complaints and pains from his not-so-spirit-feeling body.

He lay near a fire, on the other side of which Veyline sat smiling at him.

"Are you dead too?" he asked, but even as the words came out he was beginning to think that somehow he'd returned to the real world and the realm of the living.

She quirked an eyebrow. "Dead? No. Do you feel dead?"

"I feel awful."

"That doesn't surprise me given the extent of your wounds."

Perhaps he was alive after all, but he had no idea how that was possible. "I was sure I was dead."

"So was I, but you're tougher than you look apparently. By the time I got you up here, I was sure you were lost to me, but there was still life in your body. So I healed your wounds and let you rest."

"You healed me?" That didn't explain why his head was spinning or his side and back were in agony. Although all of the wounds he'd taken, at least the ones he remembered taking, seemed to be closed up and healed. "Then why do I hurt so much?"

"Could be that the healing cured your wounds, but the extent of them was such that your body still needs to recover and pain is a part of that recovery. It also could be something you did before I awoke in the middle of a flood of goblins. What exactly happened this morning?"

Pieces started to connect in Farion's mind. He smiled wearily. "I think I know why my body hurts. I'd forgotten about running flat out for miles carrying a certain mage-blade in my arms. I don't think I've pushed myself that hard in my entire life."

"Oh," was the simple reply accompanied by a wry grin. "Sorry. Why didn't you let Alred carry me? He could carry a horse without issue I think."

"Probably." Farion didn't want to explain. And after a moment of silence he went on with the rest of the story. "We woke this morning, but you didn't. It wouldn't have been an issue; we could have stayed there until you woke, but a patrol of goblins got lucky and wandered right into your shield. In the end, one of them was able to sound a horn. We knew we had to move and without your shield we had no cover, so we simply ran for it. We might have made it too if other patrols hadn't rushed out of the mountains at us. Alred, Li Tan, and I stayed behind to give the others a chance to get into the mountains and hide. Since I'd been carrying you, you were with us by proxy. After that I got the royal crap beaten out of me, and that's all I remember."

"I can pick up the story from there." She drew a long breath and let it out slowly. "I awoke as you were going down. It didn't take long to see that the situation wasn't good. The goblins were at me, and they'd separated the three of you. I protected myself as best I could. I wasn't sure I could get to everyone, so I threw a wall of fire up around you and me. That kept most of them out, and I was able to dispatch the ones inside the wall without too much trouble. Then I put a shield up around you and me and cast a handy little spell that made you, as well as your gear and mine, light as a feather and easy to carry. From there, I snuck us out of the wall of fire and up the mountainside." She paused for a long moment. "I could see the others for a while, but I couldn't help them without leaving you helpless. Then... even as I debated on going back... I saw Li Tan fall." She shook her head. "He couldn't have survived that stroke. I lost sight of Alred under swarming goblins. I assume they got him too. I brought you up the mountainside to the first safe and peaceful place I could find... here. I put a static shield up and went to work healing you. I don't think I've ever seen so many wounds on one man before. I let you rest and took advantage of that spring over there to clean myself up."

By all the gods! So that hadn't been a water nymph. Farion hoped she couldn't see his blush in the darkness.

She continued, "I remembered Orina's warning about a goblin's sense of smell and made up a little of her paste to put on. I'm glad I'd asked her what she put in it. And here we are."

Farion nodded, swallowed a lump in his throat, and found words bursting forth from his mouth. "Vey, I love you."

There was a short silence as she smiled, and it was a beautiful smile. Then she said simply, "I know."

"You do?"

The smile widened a little. "I've known for a while." She looked away and seemed to think about it for a moment. "Actually, I suspected since just after the elfin glade. But I knew that night not long ago when you were on watch and poured your heart out to me when you thought I was sleeping."

"You were awake?"

"Of course. What sort of warrior would I be if I didn't wake at the slightest touch? You put your hand on my shoulder and that woke me. I didn't feel particularly threatened, so I waited to see what would happen, who was there. Then you spoke. After that, I didn't know what to say and thought it best at the time not to destroy your illusion that I'd been asleep."

Suddenly a thousand little looks and smiles that she'd sent his way since that night made a whole lot more sense. "Oh, by all the gods."

"You're cute when you're ashamed. I'd hate to think

what you'd say if you knew I saw you watching me at the waterfall this afternoon."

Farion's mouth hung open. She knew he'd been watching! He hadn't even really known he was watching. He'd thought he was dead. By the gods! He fell back on his bedroll and groaned. She laughed a light and airy sound, full of mirth and joy.

He heard her get up, walk over, and crouch beside him. He looked the other way, not bearing to look her in the face at the moment.

Her breath on his cheek and her whispered voice in his ear sent tingles down his spine and reminded him of the day they'd met. "I love you, too." He looked at her then. Her face was close. She was still smiling, an inner light dancing in her eyes. She bent and touched her lips to his in a brief kiss.

"Now rest, my weary warrior." There were more words, whispered in some strange tongue, which he took to be magic. He fell back into a deep and restful sleep. As he did he felt her lie down next to him, very close and snug, one arm over him, another faint kiss on his cheek and then nothing.

"ake up, my weary warrior." Something hit his shoulder, jarring him into wakefulness.

Farion groaned.

He opened his eyes to find a new day well in progress, the sun high in the sky. He pushed himself up. Squinting and blinking he found the fire doused and covered over, his pack ready to go, and Vey standing beside it. Gods, but she was tall and proud and beautiful. She looked down at him with a slightly exasperated look.

She used her boot to nudge his shoulder. He assumed that's what had shocked him awake a moment before.

"Come on," she said with a playful tone. "It's not like you were beaten to within an inch of your life yesterday or anything."

He got to his feet slowly, noticing as he did that even the general pounding ache of yesterday had mostly subsided. All in all, he was feeling quite good. "Did you heal me more?" he asked, collecting his bedroll.

"Maybe."

He looked up, quirking a brow questioningly.

She continued. "Well I don't want to take anything away from your manly sense of power and strength. Maybe you're just so tough that you're ready to go the day after nearly dying."

He laughed at that. "Yeah, maybe." He finished stowing his bedroll in his pack and stood up. "Where's my armor?"

"It was kind of dented and punctured. I've mended what I could with magic, but that's not really my area of expertise. You've got a mostly intact breastplate and one good shoulder guard, and the bracers and greaves are fine."

"That will have to do."

She pointed to where it was laid out, and he went to work strapping it on. She helped, hurrying things along.

"Any reason you're in such a hurry?" he asked as they finished up.

She pointed across the way to where the burned and mangled corpses of a small troop of goblins sat smoldering on the ground.

"Oh," Farion said simply.

"Patrols are all over the mountain. We're going to need to move carefully." She drew a packet of something out of her pack and dipped a finger into it. From the smell, he could tell it was Orina's paste. She began spreading it on him.

"Where are we going?"

She gave him an odd look. "To complete our mission."

He drew in a long breath. "Right. I don't suppose you happen to magically know what happened to Raithan, Orina, and Hana?"

She shook her head. "We have to assume the worst and keep going. We may be the only chance the Seven Kingdoms have left."

"No pressure."

She smiled, leaned in, and kissed him. This time the kiss lingered on his lips and he couldn't say he really minded. When she withdrew, she said, "We have to succeed for our children."

"Children?"

"Future children."

"Oh." He had to admit he liked the sound of that. Now he had to live, if only for the children. Specifically, he was looking rather forward to the making of these children.

She wiped a small bit of the paste on his nose and turned away. "Now let's get moving. Keep close, really close. If I put up a shield, it will be a small one to conserve energy."

"If? Do you have something else in mind?"

"Yes, there's a much easier spell that senses life around me. Since we don't have Orina scouting for us anymore, I'll have to rely on that. If any patrols are getting close, I'll put the shield up."

He put a hand on her shoulder, partly to reassure her —and himself—and partly to do as she said and keep close behind her. He'd never be more than an arm's length away.

That was how they made their way across the mountainside. They encountered several patrols and Farion could see that Vey was right. The goblins were certainly worked into a frenzy of diligent activity searching for any more intruders in their territory. Vey's shield kept them from being spotted and allowed them to move through open spaces without worry of being noticed. It took them most of the afternoon, combing over the mountainside, to find an entrance into the goblin king's lair.

Farion knew the legends passed down since the time of the last goblin king almost two hundred years ago and recited from the histories.

"Inside the mountain known as Silver Peak, around which the goblin hordes gathered, there's a series of caves and caverns, some natural, some carved out, which have been the home of the goblin king throughout the ages. When there's no king, it's used as goblin-neutral ground if the warring tribes ever wish a place to meet. There are many entrances, caves, and side tunnels, but they should all lead to a central cavern, a massive place with great columns throughout. At one end is the throne and the rest is flat and mostly open. Here is where the king would meet with his generals and commanders, would reign over his 'court', and would sit for as long as he was in power."

That was where they were headed; where they would find the goblin king.

When they found an entrance tunnel, it was not large: just enough room for a person to enter. Farion was a bit suspicious that there were no guards around the cave entrance, but he wasn't going to shirk a bit of good luck.

Night was setting as they moved farther in and the tunnel was already black as night. Vey turned to him in the gloom and spoke a word of magic. A sphere of light blossomed in front of them. She sent it down the tunnel before them and lit their way.

"Won't that attract attention?"

"Perhaps, but I think everyone down here will need light. From what Orina told me, goblins have exceptional night vision but can't see in complete darkness, which means one of two things. Either these tunnels will become lit at some point, or they will be carrying torches to light their way. We should have some warning of their presence. Hopefully enough for me to put my shield up."

"Makes sense."

The floating globe traveled well in front of them, lighting the way. As it turned out, they had few encounters with goblins. Once, in a large, natural cavern, they heard others approaching and Vey put her shield up. They waited for the creatures to notice her light then she sent it off quickly down a side tunnel. The goblins all rushed after it and a moment later there was silence again. It was also completely dark. Vey created another light and they moved on. In this way they explored the caverns of Silver Peak. It was impossible to determine the passage of time down in the caves and eventually, tired and possibly lost, they created a small camp. It was in another cavern of a good size. They selected a dark corner. Vey put up a static shield, put out her light, and they curled up together in the darkness.

Farion fell asleep lying next to the woman he loved, his

arm over her, letting her even breaths lull him into his dreams.

A sound pulled him from his reverie and he came awake quickly. He was about to whisper to Vey if she was awake when more noise reached his ear and he remained silent to listen.

It was a voice, someone complaining quietly. They seemed to be griping about having rammed their foot into something in the dark.

It took Farion another moment to remember he shouldn't be able to understand what they were saying… unless they weren't goblins. He listened more intently.

A slow smile grew on his face. It was Alred's voice.

"Vey!" he whispered urgently.

"I hear it." Again she'd been awake and he hadn't known. "I'm lowering the shield. Be ready, just in case."

Farion was on his feet in an instant, sword ready.

A light blossomed to life in the cavern somewhere between their corner and where the voice was coming from. What they saw was a merry sight indeed.

Alred was shading his eyes and looked startled. He didn't look very well off at all—wounds dried over with blood, arm in a sling, limping—but the three others with him did. Raithan, Hana, and Orina were blinking at the light, though it seemed to be affecting Orina the most. She shut her eyes with a grimace and threw her hands up to block the light before finally turning away.

"Farion? Vey? We thought you were dead," Alred said slowly.

"We thought the same of all of you," Vey replied. "It's good to know we were wrong."

"Indeed," came the stoic response from Raithan.

Hana, in an unusual display of emotion, ran over and threw an embrace around Vey then released her and did the same for Farion. "It's good to see you both."

"Careful," Vey said with a grin. "That's my man you're holding."

Farion saw a smile slide onto Orina's face as she slowly turned back to the light. Hana simply took a step back and looked from him to Vey. "Did you...? Do you...? Are you two...?"

"Yes," Farion said, putting the questions at an end. "We are... if we can find the damned goblin king, kill him, and get out past hundreds of thousands of goblins."

"That's the rub." Raithan sighed. "We've been in these caves for two days now and I'm sure we've been walking in circles." This said with a sidelong look at Orina.

"We have not," Orina insisted with a small pout.

"How could I know? We've been in the dark the whole time." Raithan's tone was harsh.

"Yes," Vey said with a note of curiosity. "How have you been moving around in the dark?"

Orina said, "My senses are exceptionally keen. Though I can't see in pitch black, I can get... impressions of what's around me. That, along with my hearing and scent, have led us this far."

"To wherever we are."

"It's not my fault that I don't know where we're going. I

must inspect the tunnels methodically until we find our destination."

"That's what you say."

"Because it's the truth."

"Oh, stop it, you two!" Hana looked like she'd been hearing this for some time and had had enough. "You're not helping anything by arguing."

That stopped them. Raithan scowled, his jaw tight. Orina was still pouting. Farion smiled, for it was the first time he'd seen the family resemblance in them.

"Let me take a look at your wounds," Vey said going over to Alred.

"If you can do for me what you did for him, I'll be fine," Alred said, nodding to Farion. "I saw you stabbed through the back with a sword. I was sure you were dead."

"So was I," Farion said quietly.

"I'll see what I can do, but I may not be able to do as much; I had to sleep for half a day after I finished with that wound magnet over there."

Farion came over as she studied the big man's wounds. Alred looked bad; there was no doubt. How he was still up and going was a mystery. He was covered in blood, though there was no way to tell how much of it was his and how much was goblin. One eye was swollen shut with a nasty gash above it. There were numerous small scrapes and bloody little cuts all over the big man's face and arms. When Vey touched the arm in the sling, the Avdalander flinched with a groan.

"Broken," she muttered and continued her work.

There was a thick bandage around the leg Alred was

favoring; it was soaked through with blood. When Vey pulled it back, a large, oozing wound lay beneath.

There were other wounds as well, but none of them seemed as serious. How the big man had taken only this much was a mystery to Farion.

"We Avdalanders are made of stern stuff," he said, almost as if he'd heard Farion's thoughts.

"You must be," Vey answered, finishing her evaluation. "I lost sight of you under a heap of goblins as I escaped the fray with this one." She jerked a thumb in Farion's direction and then led Alred toward the corner of the cave where she and Farion had set up their little camp.

Alred told his story as he limped along slowly. "The goblins got it in their heads that if they swarmed me that would take me down. That's probably what saved me. That close they could use little but their claws. I went down sure enough under that pile, but I just started grabbing one at a time and ending them. By the time I was done with that, most of the rest had passed by. I staggered to the nearest cave and collapsed in the darkness. That's where these three found me and bandaged me up. I thank all the gods they found me before any goblins did. Then Ori gave me something that sure perked me up and got me on my feet again, but I'm starting to feel pretty tired again."

"Maybe you should all rest, then," Vey said. "I can do a full healing on this bigger-wound-magnet and we can take some time to regroup. It's not like the goblin king is going anywhere."

"Not a bad idea," Raithan conceded.

Farion and Vey led the others to their little corner, and

Vey put up a new static shield that would encompass all of them. Then she got Alred lying down, put him to sleep with a word, and began healing him. Once done, she rolled onto her bedroll and slept herself. The other three followed suit; they all looked tired. Without Vey's shield, they would have had to be extremely vigilant and aware all the time in these caves to avoid goblin attention. Farion was well rested and sat on his bedroll, looking into the darkness and thinking.

Mostly he wondered what this goblin king would be like. He had to be powerful in some respect or all the warring tribes wouldn't have gathered under his control. Would he have many guards? Did goblins possess any magic? Not a lot was known about these strange, war-crazed humanoids.

"Someone is coming," Orina whispered next to his ear.

Farion nearly jumped out of his skin.

"Stop that!" he breathed back.

She just laughed lightly.

He hadn't known how long he'd sat there thinking, but it seemed that the small woman had not rested long. A moment later he heard what she had and appreciated how good her hearing was. It began as just the faintest hint of sound. Only a few moments later did it become distinguishable as many footfalls. He didn't need to ask how she'd heard it before him. He already knew her senses were exceptional.

They both knew it had to be goblins, lots of them, headed this way.

Had the enemy somehow found out where the

companions were gathered? Did they have some magic none of the group knew of?

He stood and drew out his sword. "Wake the others."

"No."

"What?"

"They won't find us. Let the others rest. I don't think I could wake Vey or Alred anyway."

"Good point."

"Sit down. As long as we're in the shield, we'll be fine."

"How can you be sure?"

"I can't, but I'm fairly certain they're not coming for us. And if they're going where I think they're going this may actually be useful."

"What do you mean?"

"You'll see, just wait."

Then the noise was upon them, the repetitive crunch of many booted feet. It was absolutely terrifying, such noise in the dark and not knowing where they were going or what they were doing. He thought it couldn't get any louder, but it did. Perhaps it was some trick of the caverns, an echo or some such phenomenon, but the sound grew and grew until it was deafening.

The cavern was filled with it, seeming to shake from the level of noise. Farion was sure the beasts must be right on top of them. His heart raced and he held his sword ready in a sweaty palm. Fighting blind against an opponent who could move easily through the dark was not a pleasant thought.

The crashing, clanking stampede continued. Farion waited for that fateful and unforeseen strike from the darkness that would take him. He swallowed hard, or tried to... his mouth was dry.

On and on it went, the clamor filling his soul and tainting it with dread.

So long it lasted and then slowly died down just as it had come.

As it finally faded, something occurred to Farion. "I thought goblins couldn't see in the dark?" He berated himself. He'd been terrified over nothing.

"As far as I know they can't," came the reply from the darkness, but it wasn't Orina. It was Raithan.

"What was that?" came Hana's voice.

"Goblins marching through," Farion answered. "Orina?"

No answer.

"She must have slept through it," Raithan said.

"No, she was speaking to me before the noise came. She heard it first."

"Oh, then I have no idea where the infernal child is... blasted darkness."

"I'm sure wherever she went, she'll be back soon." Farion didn't think the little elf would simply abandon them.

"True, she's known to wander off," Hana said, and a shuffling in the darkness from where her voice had come signified movement. "I'm going back to sleep. Let me know if she finds anything interesting."

Raithan grumbled and then let out a long, aggravated sigh and shuffled off as well, leaving Farion alone in the darkness.

Farion sighed and sat.

It was some time later when Orina's voice in his ear nearly scared him out of his skin... again. "I found him."

After several calming breaths, Farion asked, "Who did you find and where did you go, and while we're at it, how can goblins see in the dark? I thought they needed light."

"I'm guessing they only need light if they don't know where they're going. But if it's a common route and they're following a strong scent, they wouldn't. Now shut up and let me speak."

Farion kept his mouth shut... for now. After a moment she continued. "It was actually the fact that they weren't using any light that tipped me off." Farion wanted to ask what she had been tipped off to but kept silent. "They must have known where they were going. I was guessing that the place they were going, the place they knew how to get to so well they could do it with their scent and hearing alone, was the hall of the goblin king." Her voice raised in pitch. "And I was right! I know where to go now!"

"Oh." That was good news.

"Come on, let's wake the others and—"

"Hold up a moment, Orina, we aren't going anywhere right now. Vey won't wake until she's ready—we've already learned that lesson—and Alred needs what rest he can get."

"Right."

"You can either wait here quietly or go scout some more."

"Right, I'll go scout." He could hear the impatient excitement in her voice. "Oh, and Farion? I'm glad you and

Vey finally talked. You don't know how much of a pain it was going back and forth between you two, listening to both of you go on about the other or watching your supposedly hidden glances in the other's direction."

"Wait, you knew how she felt?"

"Didn't you?"

"No."

"Oh... life must be difficult for you humans."

"You have no idea."

There was no response; she was off into the darkness once again.

12

E ventually Farion fell asleep. He must have because someone was calling his name and shaking him awake. It was Vey.

"You're awake," he said, groggy.

"Very perceptive."

"Don't mock me. I've been awake for all of three seconds!"

"Fair enough. Yes, I've had my beauty sleep, as has Alred, though he's still an ugly brute. We're ready to go. How're you feeling?"

"Sleeping on stone is not my thing."

"Well, if Orina is right and the goblin king is nearby, then hopefully you won't have to much longer; we'll either be out of here or dead."

"I would prefer option *A*."

"I think we all would. Are you ready to go, my love?"

"That sounds so good when you say it, and yes, I'm ready." Indeed, if the goblin king was near and some epic battle was ahead, then he could die happy knowing she loved him. Not that he wanted to die. Knowing she loved him gave him the greatest reason of all to live.

He picked himself up, gathered his things, and was soon in his armor. Vey had provided light for them to prepare by and would continue to do so as they moved through the caves protected by her shield. Orina said the Hall of the Goblin king wasn't far and there were many places to hide once they were there, but making sure they got there unseen would be important. Vey explained everything to him as he donned his armor and then they were off.

Orina led them out of the cavern, down a tunnel and then another and another, turning seemingly at random. It would have taken them some time to search all this. Orina stayed inside Vey's shield as she led them so she could explain what they would find once they got to the cavern.

"It's large, and the sides are still natural rock, but the middle is all carved out with grand pillars supporting the high ceiling. The king's throne will be ahead and to the right when we enter. There are several wide pillars we can use as cover as we approach it, or we may want to skirt around the wall for a while and keep to the shadows. The area around the throne is lit by magic globes, much like Vey uses, which I'm assuming are permanent. I wasn't able to get close to the king, but I could hear him speaking to the assembled goblins. He was telling them that they need not fear the intruders harming him as he is invincible."

"So he knows we're coming," Raithan interrupted.

"That does seem likely after the fiasco on the hill," Hana said.

"Anyone else worried about the 'invincible' part?" Farion asked. They all stared at him. "What?"

"All the other Goblin kings have died just fine," Raithan said.

Orina cleared her throat. "As I was saying, the king told his generals to keep doing their jobs and amassing their armies and then head to the human realms as soon as they were ready to march. After that, everyone left. I don't know if the king has any personal guards or who else might be patrolling these tunnels. I suggest extreme caution as we approach."

"Would it be possible to get behind him, assuming he's on the throne?" Raithan asked.

"Possibly. That would involve skirting around the wall for a while, but it could be done. We'd probably want to confirm he's actually there first before we sneak up on nothing."

"Fair enough. Can you do that?"

"Yes."

"Once we're in, confirm he's there then return to us. We'll move along the wall until we're behind him and approach from there. Hopefully we can surprise him."

"Hopefully," Orina nodded and led them on.

Shortly after, they entered the cavern. It was as massive as all the tales told, a place of dim light and many shadows. Farion could see some light farther into the cavern to their right, but not the source of it. Too many pillars stood between them, each massive in girth, casting shadows in a hatchwork over the walls and the smooth stone floor.

They immediately slipped along the wall to the right as Orina darted out from Vey's shield, moving inward from shadow to shadow.

They waited moment by moment after she had disappeared. Farion's heart raced. This was it, the culmination of their mission. Then, in the next instant, his heart fell as a great voice rang out throughout the cavern.

"Hello youngling. Come out of the shadows." The voice didn't sound like any goblin Farion had ever heard. Their voices were gravelly and guttural. This one was light and smooth but still strong and commanding. The goblin king's next words froze Farion to the bone. "The rest of you might as well join her. Your magic can't hide you from me."

They all looked at each other with expressions varying from confusion to shock and despair. At least that answered the question of whether or not the goblin king had magic.

They all stood frozen for another moment or two uncertain what to do.

"Come now Legate Raithan Haldar, such indecision is unlike you. Come out from your shield and face me."

"How does he know...?" Raithan whispered.

"Your name?" the voice finished. "I know everything about you. I know everything about all of you. I know of Alred Kuronsen's fear of rats, such small things for such a large man to fear. I know of Hana Alaui's mother and how she died and where." Hana's eyes went wide, her face draining of all color. "I know of Farion Quin and Veyline

Pristal and their new love, how tender and sweet. I know you're all here to kill me, but you might as well come out and face me for I have something to tell you before you attempt such a foolhardy act."

Raithan sighed heavily. "Everyone stay alert for any opening. Watch him like a hawk and keep an eye on each other. We may need to communicate with little or no words so be ready for anything. Vey lower your shield and let's go meet this thing that knows so much about us."

Vey nodded. "The shield is down."

Farion drew in a long breath and moved into the room with the others.

They met up with Orina, who was still hiding in the shadows of a great pillar nearer to the center of the vast cavern. Her eyes were wide and her look questioning, incredulous.

"Come, let's meet the goblin king as honorable warriors," Raithan said to his daughter. The steel and determination in his voice were admirable considering.

She drew in a long breath, shook her head in disbelief, and joined them as they all came into the light.

The central aisle of the hall was about fifty feet wide and lined with two rows of the massive pillars. High up on each pillar, suspended by nothing but air, hung the glowing orbs. The light they cast upon the hall was bright white. About two hundred feet away was a three-foot-tall rough-hewn stone dais and on it a great throne, also carved of stone. Sitting on the throne was a powerfully built and commanding-looking goblin with a crown of stone and gems on his head. The crown looked immensely heavy. The goblin king rose from the throne and beckoned them forward with a slow wave of his hand.

There were no other goblins in the room; it was deserted except for the companions and the king. It was odd and Farion hoped it was a sign of the goblin king's arrogance, not his true power, that he felt he could face them with no minions around.

They moved without haste, all of them alert and looking around and at each other for any sign or danger or action.

"I won't harm you," the goblin king said evenly. The light and airy voice seemed discordant coming out of the mouth of the creature before them. The strong, commanding tone fit, but the pitch and tenor of the voice were all wrong. "Perhaps you'd be more comfortable if I showed you my true form."

Farion stopped at this, looking to the others with a raised brow, but the rest all seemed just as confused. He looked back to the goblin king. The king's form shimmered for a moment then faded, and another figure stepped out of the shimmering disguise.

Now the voice fit the body. He was tall, taller than his previous form. It was hard to tell his height exactly from this distance. He seemed as if he could be as tall as Alred, though that was where the similarity in their two forms stopped. The king was lean and willowy, with long, thin arms, slender legs, and an impossibly lean and slight torso. His features were hard to make out from where Farion stood, but his hair was raven black with a sheen of blue and contrasted with his pale, nearly snow-white skin. His ears were quite narrow but very tall and delicate, ending in a fine point.

Farion heard someone draw in a breath and looked to see Orina, eyes wide, standing in shock. "He's syndari!"

Farion had no idea what that meant. He'd never heard the name before.

"Very good, youngling. Your mother taught you well. I wouldn't have expected a tainted half-breed to be so quick of mind." The king's voice carried easily over the distance to them. "In fact I am the grandson of Synta herself; a true blood of the royal line. My name is Aeltherion. I would ask you all to bow, but I don't think you would be quick to comply."

"Who and what are you?" Raithan called out.

"Your daughter told you already, human. It's not my fault if you don't know the history of the land which your kind so ruthlessly invaded."

Orina was quick to overcome her shock and spoke with haste. "The syndari are a race like elves. We come from the same ancient ancestors. They are the keepers of magic and lore and, as far as I knew, all lived in secluded towers studying their lives away in the far east."

"Most of us, yes." The king stepped off the three-foot platform as if it were but a normal step, seeming to float to the floor. "I've chosen to take action in the world and when a syndari decides to act it's never on a small scale." He moved toward them, gliding across the floor with smooth steps. "You're here because I've created the persona of the goblin king, but perhaps you would care to know why I did that before you attempt to kill me." He stopped about twenty feet from them a smile on his slender face that might have seemed welcoming except for his eyes, which were a clear red-orange and so intense they could almost have been smoldering. There was something powerful and deadly behind those eyes.

"Go on. Say your piece," Raithan said, still calm and in control, or at least he appeared to be.

"Obviously, I'm no goblin, nor do I care for the creatures. They've fallen so far from their ancestors that they're nothing more than an abomination now. They're a blemish on the name of Aereondai. They must be eradicated. This is why I've taken on this most disgusting of forms and assembled them all into one place. It was far too easy, really. They'll march to war at my command and throw themselves upon your human colonies wave upon wave until they're no more. So you see, you need not fear me. There's no need for your mission here. Go back to your lands and help them fight, and soon the goblin stain will be no more."

"That's monstrous!" Hana said, breathless. "Thousands, no hundreds of thousands of men and women will die!"

"And what do I care of the deaths of humans? You breed like rabbits anyway; you can always make more. I give you this warning only. When you do rebuild your kingdoms, remember the lesson of the goblin hordes and do not overstep your bounds, or perhaps I will return and do the same to you."

"You're mad." Raithan's voice was even, but for the first time, Farion thought he sensed a tremor, a hint of fear.

"Driven by a purpose you can't understand. There's a difference."

"No, you're completely mad. You can't do this."

"I certainly can and will. There's nothing you can do to stop me."

"We could do what we came to do."

Aeltherion tilted his head back and laughed. A long, loud, and unpleasant sound. The sound was so disconcerting it shook Farion to the bone. It shook them all. He could see it in the stunned and frozen expressions of disbelief on their faces. This man, or whatever he was, wasn't afraid of them in the least. When he finally regained himself he said simply, "And which one of me would you kill?"

With that Aeltherion shimmered again and a duplicate stepped out from where he'd been. Now two of the same man stood before them.

Out of the corner of his eye, Farion saw Hana raise her bow, aim, and fire in one fluid motion. There was a moment time slowed as the arrow, moving so fast across the short distance, hung in the air for what seemed like an eternity before it struck the heart of the first Aeltherion. That version screamed, head back, clutching the shaft of the arrow. The sound he made was so piercing and sharp it stunned them all once again. In the next moment, Farion thought his spine might melt as the scream became that same unnerving laughter and that version of Aeltherion regained himself with a grin.

"Wrong one," the syndari said.

Before Hana could fire again, both of the versions of

the man were shimmering and duplicating once again. This time it happened so fast as to span the breadth of a heartbeat. Then those duplicates were further dividing until, in the space of a single long breath, they were surrounded by a ring of Aeltherions, perhaps fifty or sixty or more.

"Will you kill all of me?" they asked in unison, a strange and grating noise despite the light and calm voice. "Perhaps you can all kill one of me, or ten, or a thousand if that would make you feel better." Then they all laughed, and Farion's skin crawled at the noise.

How in all the blazes of hell could they defeat a man of such power?

Then, when he was just beginning to think that all hope was lost, he felt hot breath on his ear and heard the most reassuring sound possible: Vey's voice, strong and confident, even if only the barest of whispers.

"I'm going to try something, but I'll need you to watch over me; I won't be able to protect myself until I'm done. Just keep him talking."

He turned his head and her face was just inches away. She smiled, a mischievous twinkle in her eye. Then she quickly kissed him, backed away, and sat down. She took one deep breath and then went very still.

The laughing around them stopped instantly. "What's she doing?" the Aeltherions asked as one.

"Don't you know?" Farion said with a slow smile spreading on his face. He felt more confident now than perhaps ever before in his life. Sure, he might die today, but he'd die defending his love and protecting his country.

What greater death could there be? "You seem to know everything about us. Don't you know exactly what she's doing now?"

"This magic I can't sense. It's as if she's no longer there." The Aeltherions seemed confused.

That was the first promising thing that had happened to them so far. Farion kept up the questions to distract the man and his many copies.

"How exactly do you know so much about us, anyway?"

All of the Aeltherions looked at Farion, and their eyes burned. It was no figure of speech either for the orange-red of their eyes swirled and flickered and danced, making it hard to tell exactly where the Aeltherions were looking.

"He has The Vision," Orina whispered harshly.

"Yes," the Aeltherions answered. "I can see the past and future as present. I can search through all of time and space and see the lives of all living things. I saw that your group would come for me years before you even knew of me. I knew everything about all of you before you even departed your homes. I saw how Li Tan would die. I saw the loss of the Numorian woman. I don't fear you because I've seen my own death, and it's far from here and long into the future. So you see, you've no hope of defeating me and no hope of doing anything I've not already seen."

"But you didn't see that Vey would do this, did you?" Farion knew as soon as he said it that it had been a mistake. He didn't want to draw attention back to her.

"From what I've heard of The Vision, it's never complete, especially when looking into the future, as such things are always changing with every action we and others take," Orina said accusingly.

"I'm more powerful than any seer you may have known! Do you know any of the royal blood? Do you know any that witnessed the Great Divide? I'm beyond your comprehension, half-breed!" The Aeltherions were screaming by the end of the tirade. Farion was beginning to think Raithan had been right: this man was mad. He wasn't sure if that made him feel better or worse. Madmen did crazy things; perhaps that's where the fear in Raithan's voice had come from.

"And how are we to know you are who you say you are?" Farion pushed on. "One minute you are a goblin, then a syndari, whatever that is, and then you are dozens of yourself. How do we know any of this is real? How do we know you're as powerful as you say?" This time he didn't realize his mistake until it was too late.

One of the Aeltherions fired a bolt of white burning energy at him.

It happened so fast Farion didn't even register the attack. He knew only that the air was knocked from him and he was blown back. Then there was the acrid smell of burned flesh as he slid across the stone floor. He skidded to a stop at the feet of one of the Aeltherions.

He groaned only now feeling the pain in his chest.

Lesson learned. Never challenge a madman to show you his power, or he just might... on you.

The Aeltherions were all laughing.

Farion tried to regain his breath. It wasn't easy, mostly from the burning in his chest. He gritted his teeth and rolled onto his stomach and then slowly pushed himself to his hands and knees. He would get up and show this bastard what he was made of.

But the Aeltherion nearest him stepped in and kicked him hard in the stomach. Despite the man's stick-thin legs, the kick held a supernatural strength and launched him across the cavern. He hit one of the pillars nearly ten feet off the ground. There was a sickening crack in his side as his ribs broke, and pain washed over his entire body.

Then he landed at the base of the pillar, hitting his head hard and sending his vision spinning with another wave of agony.

He couldn't even contemplate moving for a while as he simply tried to breathe without pain, only to discover he couldn't.

He faintly heard some of the Aeltherions say, "Do you doubt my power now, puny human!" while the rest continued to laugh that jarring, discordant laugh.

Ever so slowly, ever so carefully, he began to move.

He would give Vey the time she needed, distract this monster just a little longer. He got an arm under him and pushed himself up to a sitting position at the base of the pillar. Then he slowly gathered his legs and found the strength to stand, even with every movement causing searing pain throughout his body. He gritted his teeth and forced a slow grimace onto his face. He reached over his shoulder and drew his sword. The sheer weight of the heavy weapon nearly toppled him, so weak was he, but he held fast gathering his strength.

"Is that the worst you can do?" he said through his teeth.

"Farion, no!" It was Hana.

Farion was outside of the circle of Aeltherions now and staggered in a step or two before swinging his sword with all the strength he had. The attack nearly spun him off his feet, but he was successful. The head of one of the Aeltherions went flying from its body.

There was a stunned silence, but only for a moment. Then all the Aeltherions, even the head that had just been removed, commenced laughing again. One of them turned to face him.

"Do you think your weapons can do anything against me? You're a fool." With a shake of his head, which clearly dismissed Farion as a threat, that one turned back around and joined the laughter of the others.

"Nothing can stop the glory of my plan!" they shouted as one. "All the goblins will die, and there's nothing you can do! All you do is make things worse for yourselves. I'll now ensure that all of your nations pay dearly when the goblin armies swarm over you. You'll defeat them, but you'll be a shattered people. This is my decree!"

Farion lopped off the head of another one. It simply laughed at him from the floor. He looked down into its wild eyes with a grin.

"I thought you'd seen the future and it was set," Farion growled. "Now you change it so easily? Perhaps you've not seen everything. Perhaps you do die, here and now."

The laughter stopped.

Silence echoed through the cavern.

All those burning eyes turned to Farion and each of the faces was deadly serious. "No, it's you who'll die now." All of them lifted their right hand toward him and...

"See your king for what he truly is! No goblin at all!"

All eyes turned away from Farion to the fifty new arrivals: goblins, or actually, from their stature and size, hobgoblin commanders. They all looked a little stunned to be there, which Farion couldn't blame them, for they'd appeared in the room out of nowhere. Wherever Vey had plucked the hobgoblins from, she'd positioned them perfectly on the outside of the circle of Aeltherions. Now the false goblin king had enemies on both sides. The hobgoblins themselves were staring at this strange situation, weapons at the ready. Vey continued even as the Aeltherions turned to her. "Look upon the face of this mighty creature who pretends to be your king. He's just an elf, seeking to destroy you all!"

"I'm no mere elf! I'm syndari."

"Not a goblin," Vey cut in.

The hobgoblins were quick to adjust and adapt. One of them called out, "Where's our king? What have you done to him?"

"I am your king!" all the Aeltherions shouted. "Obey me or I will destroy you. Kill these human intruders, now!"

None of the hobgoblins moved.

"Now!"

One of the hobgoblins, a nasty look on his face, approached one of the Aeltherions. It got right up close, face to face. Its voice was everything Farion would expect: guttural, rough and deep. "Why would I kill worthless humans when there's syndari scum to play with? Do you think we're stupid? We know what you are, now that you have come out from hiding."

The others grunted their approval of the sentiment.

It was the most wonderful thing Farion had heard all day.

The hobgoblin's axe came up in an easy swing, cutting the Aeltherion he was talking to from hip to opposite shoulder.

Chaos broke loose.

Burning bolts of energy flew across the room from all sides, axes and blades alike began cutting down the copies of the syndari wizard. Hana's arrows flew in rapid succession, knocking down Aeltherion after Aeltherion.

Only Farion and Orina were not involved in the mess of the melee. He staggered back and leaned against a pillar, working hard simply to remain standing. He could see that Orina wasn't fighting and wondered why. She seemed to be looking keenly into the corners of the room or cocking her head as if to listen better over the din of combat.

Farion knew he would never hear what she was listening for, but he began to look around as well. Just looking at Orina made him feel that something wasn't right. He glanced from side to side into the shadows of the room but saw nothing. He kept looking, peering into the gloom at the edges of the room.

Then he saw it... or did he?

A flicker of something. A shade of deeper darkness within the shadows.

There was someone there—a tall, slender form almost completely obscured in the dimness at the edge of the room.

The shadowed form was on the other side of the melee. Farion was looking right past Orina, who stood still as a statue in the middle of the battle. She looked at him from the side of her eyes, meeting his gaze. Then she glanced back toward what he'd seen, the shadow and then back to him as a smile crept onto her face with the faintest of nods.

Orina turned, raised her bow, notched an arrow, and released it all in one liquid, graceful movement.

At the same time, a blossom of light from the darkness in that shadowed corner shot forth toward them all.

Time slowed once again.

Farion watched the arrow cut through the air into the shadows. It slipped right past the growing blast of energy and hit solidly, sinking into its nearly imperceptible target. It hit as the bolt of light struck Orina. All the Aeltherions cried out at once and shimmered to nothing as a blast of super-heated energy exploded on the elf, washing a wave of force over all of them.

Farion was smashed back into the pillar once more, collapsing, but as he sunk into the blackness of unconsciousness he heard a scream of agony, disbelief, and hatred from that dark corner. Then there was nothing.

13

Once again voices intruded on his deep and comforting darkness.

"What the hell did he do? He looks like he's been dragged into the flames of the burning abyss and back." It was a concerned voice. A female voice. It was a voice he knew, a voice that gave him great comfort even if he couldn't identify it at the moment.

"He did what you told him to do," a gruff male voice said. "I overheard your little talk with him before you did your thing. He kept the insane and powerful wizard occupied. Mostly by allowing the insane and powerful wizard to beat the crap out of him."

"I love him, but he really doesn't seem that bright sometimes."

"He did what he had to do."

"And that's why I love him."

"Now heal him enough to walk, but not so much that you can't walk, before those hobgoblins wake up and decide we're a good second course for their fighting appetites."

"Point taken."

Then warmth flooded into him. It was comforting and soft, like being wrapped in a heavy blanket on a cold day.

He drew a long breath, which hurt like hell, and opened his eyes.

Vey was there, her face inches from his.

"Hello, wound magnet."

"Hi." His voice was hoarse and hollow. "I don't sound good. Come to think of it, I don't feel too good, either."

"Can you walk?"

"I think so."

"Then you feel good enough." She helped him up and indeed his legs were strong enough to support him, but he still felt like a herd of horses had trampled him with flaming hooves.

He looked around. It was a grim sight. They were all battered and a little singed. The hobgoblins were still out cold and Farion had no idea why his companions were up so quickly, but he smiled at that bit of luck.

Then the smile slid off his face as he saw Raithan carrying something. It was a small, blackened form.

Vey caught the glance. "Orina didn't make it."

The look on Raithan's face was hard to read. The man's jaw was clenched, his eyes were hard, but there was a line from his eye down his cheek where the soot had been washed away.

"Come on," Alred said, trotting over. "We need to move now."

They all started moving toward where they'd entered the cavern.

"Is Aeltherion dead?" Farion asked.

It was Hana who responded, nodding. "He's dead. Alred and I found the body in that dark corner. Orina paid the ultimate price, but she made sure we got him. The real him."

Vey nodded. "Plus, I doubt any goblin or hobgoblin is going to trust anyone who claims to be a goblin king anytime soon. The threat is gone. Believe it or not, we succeeded."

"Fair enough."

They left the cavern by the same tunnel that had led them in, but even with Vey's light they didn't know the way out. It was Orina who'd gotten them in here and none of them could seem to recall the exact series of tunnels they'd taken. They were soon lost in the labyrinth of tunnels leading to the surface.

They stopped eventually, mostly for Farion. Vey did a little more healing on all of them. Then they slept.

14

It was three more days before they reached the surface—a day being the length of time between sleeping. When they emerged from the mountain, there was chaos in the valleys below.

"Good," Raithan said, his voice still heavy. "They're already breaking up. They won't be a threat for much longer." He still carried Orina; it was his burden. He'd wrapped her in a blanket and carried her in his arms like a swaddled baby. He'd said he would bury her as soon as they reached the forest that had been her home. He could give her that much.

They made their way slowly back across the ridge where things had fallen apart on their way in. The goblins now seemed more interested in fighting amongst themselves and gathering as much loot as they could. They encountered a few stray war-bands, but nothing they couldn't defeat or avoid with Vey's shield. It took them another two full days to cross the ridge because they were moving so carefully. This brought them back to where Storm was tethered. It was around noon on a dark and rainy day. It was a warm rain, being the height of summer, but the wetness and dreariness of the day seemed to set their mood. They might have succeeded, but even with the victory, the cost to the party had been high.

Farion offered to have Storm carry Orina, but Raithan refused.

Disheartened and dour, they simply made camp where Storm had been, resting the remainder of the day.

Farion took Storm for a little walk around and told his equine friend about all the things that had happened while he'd been away. Storm whinnied and nickered at the appropriate points, even nuzzling Farion's shoulder when the knight told him of the deaths of Li Tan and Orina.

"I don't know what will happen now old friend, but I know I've got someone else in my life." Storm whinnied. "Oh don't be that way. You know you're always first in my life. There's just someone who's second now, where there wasn't before. Things are going to change, but don't you worry. I get the feeling you'll be getting lots of exercise for some time to come, riding me back and forth to Elrios."

There was a break in the rain, and Farion looked up to see a crack of blue sky between the dark clouds. He smiled then and led Storm back to the camp.

15

Two days later, they were back in the Everrun Forest.

It was a beautiful day with the sun filtering down through the foliage above.

They found a clearing with a patch of sunlight and a sapling growing at the center. They buried Orina there, Vey using her magic to cover the grave in such a way as to make it seem as if the earth had never been disturbed. There might still be many goblins filtering through the area in the next while and they wanted to ensure no goblin or scavenger disturbed this place.

Raithan stood there for some time at the foot of the grave, simply looking down at the barest of mounds. Orina was so small she hadn't displaced much earth. He stood, saying nothing, or perhaps saying many things privately to his daughter. Finally, he spoke up.

"I never understood you." He looked away from the grave then to any other place. "And I don't know if you ever understood me." Another pause where he couldn't bear to look at his daughter's burial place. "But..." His voice was strained now and became quiet. "I loved you and... and I think you loved... all of us in your own distant way. You saved our lives more times than I probably know, and your skill at scouting and in battle was amazing, unsurpassed. And in the end, when it came to it, you sacrificed yourself for us, the noblest act of a warrior. We may never have seen eye to eye, but I think... I think now I understand you a little more. I think now I understand your heart. The heart of a warrior." His voice was fully choked up now and he stopped, turned away, striding to the edge of the clearing. No one followed.

They all had their own private words to say, and when it was Farion's turn he stood at the foot of the grave and smiled.

"You were so young, but I think you were the wisest person I'd ever met. You told me to stop being an idiot and say what was in my heart. It took me far too long to do that, to even understand that, but I thank you for it. Then there was the saving of my life. I owe you everything really. I'll have to talk to Vey and all, but I think if we ever have a girl, we'll call her Orinarra. I will never forget you little one." Now he was getting choked up, tears in his eyes. There were more words, but they all seemed useless now. He smiled through his tears, unable to speak. He knelt to lay a hand on the earth, then rose and simply said, "Goodbye."

16

"I think it's perfect," Vey said as they walked down a long, slow slope on a simple road leading to the Quin family holdings.

Farion, after months of being away, was nearly home. He had the woman he loved by his side, and it was a beautiful early fall day. It had taken him this long to work up the courage to ask Vey about kids and tell her his idea about naming their daughter after a certain half-elf.

"I'm glad you like it."

She smiled and linked her arm in his as they walked, Storm a few steps behind. "I don't think Li Tan would be a good name for our son, though."

"No? Why not?"

"A little too foreign. Orinarra doesn't sound like any names from the Seven Kingdoms, except maybe Numoria. Li Tan is definitely Tianese. People might get confused."

"I could see that. What about Laitan or Laithan?"

"Now it sounds like you're trying to name our kid after Raithan."

Farion laughed. "Not my first choice, but I've come to respect the name."

"True. Laithan isn't bad, but we have lots of time to decide. No kids on the way yet."

"We're not getting any younger," Farion said and gave her a quick playful kiss on the cheek.

"True, perhaps we can get started... soon. How far away are your estates? A soft, warm bed might go a long way toward tempting me to... practice."

Farion smiled. They were on their way up another slope. He took his time answering, drawing out his words. "It should be just... over this... hill," he finished as they crested the small rise. More rolling plains fell away from them.

Vey looked around. "I don't see anything."

"This land is all mine, or my family's at least. Another couple of hours will bring us to the Eastern House. My family is usually in the West this time of year, so we'll have it mostly to ourselves."

"Sounds pleasant."

"I thought so."

They continued walking down the other side of the hillock.

After a while, Vey spoke, her tone serious. "What's next for us, Farion?"

He stopped and turned to her. "What do you mean?"

She sighed. "There are so many questions to answer. Where will we live? When and where is the right time for kids? And what's next? Are we both just going to give up our ways and settle down? Something about that just doesn't feel right to me." Her almond-colored eyes gazed into his.

He drew in a long breath. "You're right, of course." He thought about it a moment and offered his arm to continue walking. She took it and they kept going.

"Li Tan said he was the leader of some rebellion in Tian. That means... now they'll be leaderless. We could always offer our services."

"I don't know the first thing about Tian or its people or culture.

Farion grinned, and he looked at her sidelong. "Then I suppose the question is..." A wide smile spread onto that beautiful face of hers, full of mischief and excitement as if she already knew what he was going to say. "...How much do you want to find out?"

THE SWORDMASTER'S APPRENTICE
A Tale of the Seven Kingdoms

Alone and hunted in an uncaring country...

Orinarra has always been able to look after herself, but after her swordmaster instructor is murdered and assassins pursue her relentlessly, she's forced to turn to the only person she trusts, her brother.

When Leethan answers his sister's desperate summons, he finds himself mired in political machinations far deeper than he could have imagined. They're caught in a web of corruption in a country on the edge of civil war.

Together they must solve the mystery of who killed Orinarra's teacher and, in doing so, fight to overthrow an entire government. Despite all their training, they are still untested and both fear they'll fail, causing this kingdom to fall into chaos.

CHAPTER 1

L eethan pulled the hood of his cloak down over his face and pushed into the crowded tavern.

The stench of sweat and beer washed over him. A few dozen voices talking and shouting mingled into an echoing din.

Over the noise came a high, young voice. "Can I take your cloak, sir?" Some barmaid wanted to be courteous.

He shook his head and waved her away. Things would go easier for him if no one in the bar saw his face, of that he was fairly sure.

His height alone made him stand out in Therra and his darker skin would instantly give him away as Elriosan. His father was Lorestin, but he took more after his mother with her dark bronze skin.

He smiled and closed his eyes incanting a quick spell of Life-Sense. Even with his hood down and eyes closed, he knew where everyone was around him. The simple magic gave him a perfect sense of the position, movement, and size of all life around him, from the smallest ant in the straw strewn over the floor to the big bartender. He easily navigated the room to the bar.

Without looking up, he signaled the bartender. The man hesitated then made his way over. The large man, who smelled of stale beer and spirits, kept ducking and leaning to see who was under the cowl, but Leethan was well hidden.

"Sir?" the man asked, unsure.

"I'm looking for someone."

"Yes?"

"A woman about this tall." He indicated with his hand. "Blond hair, bronze skin, calls herself Orina, or just Ori."

"Oh, yes, yes, I know her. What's your business with the young lady?"

"My business is none of yours." Leethan took a thick gold coin from a pouch at his belt and laid it on the counter. "All you need to do is tell me where she is."

"I... I uh... I don't know where she is right now, but perhaps I can tell her where to find you?" As he said this, the man moved his head to look up and to the side, unaware that Leethan could sense his every move. There were rooms on the second floor of the tavern and Leethan had strong reason to suspect that Ori was here.

He drew the coin back. "Your loss. I'll just go check upstairs if you don't mind."

"You can't do that, sir, those rooms are private, for guests. I can't..." The man blustered on while Leethan sighed and concentrated the few heartbeats it took him to cast a quick mental control spell. It wasn't powerful, but it would work.

"I'll take a look upstairs if you don't mind." The spell was woven into the last three words.

"I don't mind," the bartender said.

"Good." Leethan made his way to the stairs and up to the second floor.

His Life-Sense spell could pick out specific life signatures which were known to him, but usually he had to be close. How close depended on how long he had been around a person previously and how long it had been since he'd seen them. Ori's particular bio-signature was well known to him, but he hadn't seen her in years. He walked down the upper hall until he felt hers in a room to the left. She was with someone... more than just with... very, very close to them. There was a larger life-sign on top of her on the bed in her room. There were various sounds and grunts coming from the other side of the door.

Leethan sighed. "Ah, come on Ori, really?" He paused, definitely not wanting to walk in on his sister in the middle of... doing what she was doing.

Then he heard a sharp cry that didn't sound like pleasure at all. He focused his Life-Sense on the two and realized that it wasn't what he had thought.

Someone was attacking Ori.

He kicked the door open and ran into the room. He incanted a quick spell of paralyzation and released it on Ori's attacker.

The man froze, and with a kick from underneath, she tossed him onto the floor.

"There are more!" she hissed, rolling out of bed. She wore a shift, and her short blond hair was tousled. She hardly spared a look at him. Instead, she drew her sword from its sheath.

Another form in dark clothing slid in through the window. Ori was quick, stabbing the man in the throat before he could take in the room. He dropped.

Barely audible footfalls sounded in the alley below. Leethan met Ori at the window, looking out as a third dark-clad form disappeared around the corner.

Ori slammed her palm against the windowsill.

"What?"

"I wanted one of them alive."

"He's still alive," Leethan said, pointing to the attacker he'd paralyzed, now lying awkwardly on the floor.

"Oh? Good. I didn't know what you'd done to him."

"Is this a usual night for you?"

She grimaced. "No, but things haven't been usual for some time." She studied the paralyzed man on the floor, then drew in a long breath and nodded. "All right, let me get dressed and we'll ask him a few questions." She pulled off her shift in one fluid motion.

Leethan spun back to the window, shaking his head.

"What?" He heard her voice behind him. "It's not like we didn't bathe together as kids. You've seen me naked before."

"Not... recently." Gods, did the woman have no decency? "In fact, I'm beginning to think I don't know you that well at all anymore. We haven't spoken much in the last nine years. I think I've only had one other letter from you since you came to Therra. When was that?"

"Nine months ago."

"Right. And there was no mention of any danger. Even this last one only said you were in trouble and to come at once. I didn't know trouble meant... assassins. Hell, trouble up until now meant some doting boy you couldn't get rid of."

He heard her sigh behind him. "Things have changed a bit since last we saw each other."

"That," Leethan said, eyeing the two black-clad men on her floor out of the corner of his eye. "I can see."

ALSO BY R. MICHAEL CARD

TALES OF THE SEVEN KINGDOMS

The Goblin King

The Swordmaster's Apprentice

GUARDIANS OF LIGHT

Book 1: The Last Scion

Book 2: Scion Rising

Book 3: Scion's Sacrifice

R. MICHAEL CARD

R. Michael Card has loved fantasy since he read his first Dragon Lance book so many years ago. He has been writing for twenty years but has only recently decided to start sharing his work with the world. He has always enjoyed the lighter side of epic fantasy, the grand adventure, and has infused that love into his works.

He lives near Toronto, Ontario with his beloved wife and their cat. He has had a plethora of careers, working in software, insurance, trades, and education, with jobs ranging from washing cars to career counseling.

www.ingramcontent.com/pod-product-compliance
Lightning Source LLC
Chambersburg PA
CBHW030616130626
46552CB00002B/600